CHAIN MAIL

A DARK PARANORMAL ROMANCE

THE SLEEP SAGA
BOOK 1

NANDER

Copyright © 2025 by Nander

All rights reserved.

No part of this book may be reproduced in any form or by any electronic or mechanical means, including information storage and retrieval systems, without written permission from the author, except for the use of brief quotations in a book review.

#HumanStorysOnly, no AI was used to produce this story.

Cover Art by NANDER

Written by NANDER

Proudly Self Published through Ingram Sparks

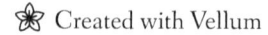

❋ Created with Vellum

*For the girls who sleep too much
and the demon who watches you do it.*

"Let her sleep, for when she wakes, she will shake the world."

—NAPOLEON BONAPARTE

NOTE FROM THE AUTHOR

Thank you so much for giving my book a chance. Chain Mail is my first dark romance, so it is not comparable to other works I have published thus far. While writing it was cathartic, editing was often morally exhausting. It contains material that may be troubling to some readers. I urge you to review the trigger warning list and consider your mental well-being before consuming this work.

This book is intended for an audience of 18+, but I understand that it may fall into the hands of someone younger. For that reason, I want to stress that while this book will romanticize an abusive dynamic and sexual assault, *nothing* about that is normal. If your partner is depriving you of basic needs, harming you, torturing you, assaulting you, or scaring you (without your consent and without a very lengthy conversation about limits, boundaries, and safe words), you are in danger. Resources for domestic violence and SA victims can be found in the afterword.

Please read this disclaimer in the double-door note.

For Non-Spicy Readers: This is a double-door book, a concept I created in my first work, Opals & a Nimbus. It allows the reader to skip triggering sexual content without missing major plot points. However, because this book is much more spice-driven than Opals & a Nimbus, skipping the doors may cause you to miss some aspects pertinent to the plot. You may need to rely on context clues or reach out on instagram. I would rather you reach out than endure a triggering, intimate scene. The doors are not full-proof and sexually aggresive scenarios may still appear on page.

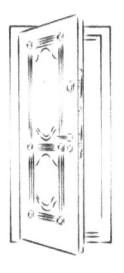

Spicy scene begins

Spicy scene ends

TIGGER WARNINGS

Haunting
Sexual Assault, Dub-con, & Rape
Sleep paralysis demon
Sleep paralysis
Somnophilia
Body mutilation
Suffocation
Sleep deprivation
Stalking
Knife play
Medical trauma
Gore and violence
Sadism & Masochism
Drug use
Profanity
Torture
Coercion
Bleeding
Assault
Biting
Choking
Homophobia
Outing
Anal
MLM & MF
Consumption of flesh
Buried alive
Annoying ass roommates

1

BANE

I stood at the foot of her bed, looking down at her. My senses told me she was falling into REM sleep. The room was blanketed in darkness, but unlike her human eyes, mine were made for the night and the night alone. She would not see me when she woke, but I could see her clearly: a twenty-something-year-old sleeping alone. Her blond hair was loosely tied up in a messy bun with a pink scrunchy. Frizzy curls of stray hair had sprung free from the small patches in front of her ears. Her face was pressed into the pillow, with a puddle of cold drool under her cheek, and she slept on her stomach with her legs open. A smile creased my face, exposing my fangs. I loved it when I landed a human who slept naked.

It was not often we touched them. Our power was limited when traveling by the Sacred Sands to the human world. Touching them took tremendous energy and shortened our stay, defeating the entire purpose of haunting. I had to control myself if I was going to get my fill. Demons like me? We thrive on human terror. Luckily, this one was young enough to terrify with ease, and I had a feeling she would be a fighter.

I crawled on the bed between her legs and pulled one cheek to the side with my thumb, grinning at her asshole. She looked tight. After the vivid dream I woke from earlier in the day, it took everything I had not to keep her asleep and fuck her. Aside from a sore ass, she would never know, but I had to be smart. Groaning, she rolled onto her back, eyes no longer dancing under her eyelids. *Must be a light sleeper.* I huffed in disappointment. *One more touch.*

I filled my palm with a large breast and gave it a few firm rubs. She drew in a breath, her eyes fluttering open. I pulled back my hand, feeling her questioning fear. Brows furrowed, she slowly lifted onto her elbows and swallowed hard.

"Hello?" she asked weakly and slowly reached her hand out. The human would not be able to see me even if her room was bright. Her hand passed through my chest, and she felt nothing but the static cold of my presence. With a gasp, she shot her hand back and brought her knees to her chest. Her breathing quickened, but she was not quite sure how scared she needed to be.

She tried hard to see in the darkness, eyes wide and darting around. They were round and green, with yesterday's mascara caked to the lashes. Her pupils were blown wide as adrenaline coursed through her. She was oblivious that I was inches from her face, trying to get another look at her chest.

Images from the latest dream I had flashed through my mind again. I only ever dreamt of one person my entire life. Over the years, my obsession with that human consumed me. Usually, the visions were of her chewing on a pencil or smoking some herb. And occasionally, I would see her bathing. But that was my first dream where she was trying to get off.

In it, she was naked, showering, and trying to touch herself. She was not good at it. I watched in frustration as her fingers wandered, occasionally putting one finger in and thrusting it unrhythmically. Eventually, she stopped, shook her head, and turned off the water. I woke up restless and hard. My lip twitched, and I swore for the millionth time that when I finally found her, she would never know peace again, not until she agreed to be mine, not until I marked her—*my little dream*.

But the girl measuring her breath in front of me was not her. She was not fair-skinned and did not have silky black hair with blue streaks or blunt bangs. She did not have my girl's edgy smile or perfect little tits. But the memory made me eager.

I grabbed her ankles hard and yanked them straight, pulling her flat on her back. She screamed once before I stopped her breath. Then I froze her. I suppose this part of the haunting is why humans call us "sleep paralysis demons." Her body could not move except for the parts I allowed.

Unlike some other sleep demons, I let my prey breathe for most of the haunting. *Most* of it. I preferred the sound of them trying to scream for help through a locked jaw. Her ample chest stopped rising, her jaw clenched shut, and her body tensed. Terror exploded inside of her, and it fueled me, but the strength it took to touch her was eating the power up faster than I could store it.

I dragged her by the ankles to the foot of the bed, letting her feet dangle by the floor. Humans were terrified of what could be lurking under their beds. The little trick worked well, and I bit my lip.

Letting go, I hovered over her and growled with pleasure, allowing her to hear what she did to me. She whimpered again.

Finally, I let her breathe. She gasped through clenched teeth. Her chest rose and fell fast, shaking her breasts. She tried to scream, but her jaw was too tight. I sent a wind up her body and could feel terror blooming in her core. My second cock, possessed by a spirit since I entered adulthood, rubbed itself against my thigh in excitement.

I was growing stronger by the minute but was far from being satiated. I watched her eyes water as she lay frozen under me. To my discontent, she did not fight it once. My entire body tingled anyway. I glanced down at her trembling chest, fighting the urge to give in for once. Her muffled screams did little to stop me.

There's a first time for everything. It was not our custom to take that much from humans. The terror of paralyzing them gave us what we needed, and taking more was in bad taste. But I could not stop trying to justify doing it and then dragging her back to the Dream World to share her with the cavern guards. So many of them forfeit their hauntings each night to serve as guardians of the Sacred Sands. *The least I can do is bring them some pleasure.* But was this human worthy of the honor of traveling to our world and sharing our beds?

Excited, my claws sprung out as I gripped the mattress. They tour through it, plush cotton erupting through the frayed holes. My cocks twitched. *Control yourself.* In my position, it would set a dangerous precedent. I had to get a grip. I closed my eyes to avoid the temptation of her body trembling violently. I was almost done with her, my energy reserves climbing, body healing, and bulb now painfully full of fresh seed.

But then, the gauges in my ears echoed. I cringed at the

abruptness of it. I could hear a voice from somewhere distant. It was annoying and preppy, causing me to grind my fangs against each other. My lip twitched at the realization. I was being summoned.

This better not be another high school sleepover. I unfroze the human under me. She shrieked, scrambling to the top of her bed and hugging her knees to her chest. She sobbed uncontrollably, rubbing her sore jaw and catching her breath. I glared at her from across the bed, like a lion watching its dinner get away. My eyes fell on her pussy. I haunted her harder than most, yet she had not gotten wet from it. *Humans are so fucking strange.*

I held out a hand. "Sleep," I muttered too low for her to hear. The weak human dozed off quickly. Her body fell limp, and her head thumped against the wall. I sucked my teeth in disappointment. *I thought she was going to be a fighter.*

I rolled my shoulders, standing up and closing my eyes to focus on the voice that summoned me. Duty called. If we terrorized the humans for our gain, it came with a price: They called? We came to them with haste. Very rarely were we beckoned by a practiced witch with a worthy errand, but not even my rank could get me out of it. The timing of it was odd, though. It was not often a demon would be chosen to answer a summoning while they were haunting. As a rule, sustaining ourselves took priority.

Nevertheless, I tuned into the voice. My mind's eye searched through time and space to find it. I went with ease, and the room slowly took shape from the swirling gray smoke of my travels. There was more than one person there, and they were giggling. But aside from them, I felt an unusual presence—a *significance*—in the room. It was courageous and bold but naive to true terror. It was captivating. I looked around as the new space continued to take shape, searching for the source.

What I saw made adrenaline rush through my body. Ivory and silver formed between the three giggling girls. My eyes grew wide. A smile creased my face. I was not being summoned with some low novelty store Ouija board. No. *This* was The Ivory Board. *This* was a high board. It would never choose a demon at random; only a high board could summon a specific demon. If the humans using it did not summon someone in particular, it chose the best demon for the job.

Despite the three trifling girls who had somehow gained possession of such an important artifact, I was here for a significant reason. *They* were *not* it. *They* were not the source of the intoxicating presence I felt. They were not the source of the voice I heard just then, which made my heart leap in predatory excitement. I knew this voice. My lips twitched. My eyes searched through the swirling gray smoke, hunting for her.

The smoke around them turned into a bed. Then, the floor became visible. There was a desk, and on it was a transparent, blue box that glowed on one side. The walls took shape, covered in posters. The smoke receded into the corners, revealing another bed. Time slowed until the last of the vapor vanished. At last, the dimly lit room was clear, and I could see why I was called here.

Sitting apart from the group, face glowing in the artificial light of the blue box, was *her*, and a rabid obsession consumed me.

My little dream. I found you, and you will never escape me.

2

BUFFY

EARLIER THAT DAY

"Albert Einstein didn't have more neurons than the average person either!"

I tapped my pencil on the table, waiting for Mr. Feeny to clean the wet-erase marker off the overhead projector slide. This lecture on the human brain was interesting, but he was slow. I loved my college Anatomy and Physiology class and couldn't have gotten luckier with my professor. I sighed quietly and fumbled with my key ring, taking a moment to feed my Giga Pet.

"In fact, class, the only difference they found between the brain of an average thirty-year-old man and the brain of Albert Einstein was that he had significantly more *glial* cells. Glial cells are *support* cells. Without them, the neurons could not function at their optimal capacity. Does anyone here know *how* you would get more glial cells?" he inquired, smiling under his salt-and-pepper mustache.

My Giga Pet clinked against the desk, and I raised my hand.

"Yes, Buffy."

"Studying or challenging your brain. Learning new things. The text references nuns who studied the Bible their whole lives and had an excess of glial cells, too."

"Precisely! This could mean reading a new book, doing crossword puzzles every morning, or even simply trying a new food. Now, one thing they find in many dementia patients is a lack of supporting cells and an excess of *plaque*."

The sound of twenty-five binders snapping shut and notebooks sliding off tables filled the air. Mr. Feeny turned to the clock. The class was over in thirty seconds.

"Don't forget to read chapter thirty-six and do the post-chapter questions. Some of them may make a guest appearance on your exam," he said, drying the plastic slide.

I tucked my long black hair behind my ear as I rose from my desk, and a few shoulders bumped me as I walked through the crowded doorway. It was my last class of the day, so I decided to head back to my dorm and finish my reading assignments.

I pulled my headphones on and carefully placed Korn's new Follow the Leader album in my CD player. My baggy JINCO jeans dragged on the ground, wearing down the fabric at my heels and getting wet in the puddles. The back pockets were big enough to fit my CD player in them, and if I walked slowly enough, the CD wouldn't skip.

It was hot, and I could feel the sun's heat absorbing into my jet-black hair, making sweat pebble on my pale forehead under my blunt bangs. I picked up my pace, weaving in and out of the mass of horny, anxious students. My dorm was on the other side of campus, and unfortunately, my backpack was heavy as hell.

Skeeter nodded his head toward me, but I pretended not to see. He was cute, with black liberty spikes and a lip ring. But otherwise, he wasn't my type. He talked... *a lot,* and it was usually about himself.

Come to think of it, none of the guys at the college were my type. The few hookups I had in my life left me confused about why people loved sex so much. The first time was painful and quick. When I tried it a few more times with different partners, Skeeter regrettably being one of them, it was fast and confusing.

What can I say? It was simply a thing that happened and usually resulted in them wanting to spend the night. But my dorm room bed was small, and I got hot at night. I hated having a warm body in my space. Especially a sweaty one that came all over my sheets while leaving me wondering what an orgasm felt like or if I'd ever have one.

I opened my dorm room door, and a wall of cold air hit me. That would have lifted my mood if it weren't for the sight of Tommy's bare ass as he fucked Neveah on my bed. I pulled my headphones off by their plastic band. The sound of Falling Away from Me blasted through the earpieces as my mouth hung open.

"What the fuck, dude?"

They scrambled apart, Neveah giggling and Tommy guarding his junk. I turned my face, rolled my eyes, and slammed the door.

"On my bed? *Really?* That's so grody, Neveah. You're washing my sheets."

"Sorry, Buff. We just got caught up in the moment," Tommy explained as he zipped up his pants and looked around. I spotted two collared shirts on my dorm mate's bed, grabbed them, and threw them at his face. Neveah was pulling her spaghetti strap top over her massive breasts when he finished popping both collars and kissed her.

"Come over; let's finish this at my place."

"'Kay! Let's bounce. Girls' night starts soon," she enthused, looking up at him under frosted, baby-blue eyelids.

Tommy was out the door before she was. She passed me, mouthing "sorry" in the most disingenuous way. Chewing her gum like a freaking horse, she smoothed her chunky blond highlights and zigzag parted locks and skipped out after him.

My eyes rolled at the sight of her neon G-string above her hip huggers as she pranced down the hall. I slammed the door shut, walked to my bed, and threw my bag down. That's when I noticed a giant box on the floor. It had a Post-it note stuck to it.

To my beautiful girl,
Good luck with finals, Jellybean.
-Mom

I tipped the box on its side and drew in an excited breath.

"No way!" I shrieked, ripping open the box of the iMac G3. I pulled it out, noticing the clear plastic monitor. It was royal blue—my favorite color—and matched the chunky highlights in my hair.

I got to work setting it up immediately, pushing Neveah's condom wrapper and Cosmo magazines out of the way. It took up quite a bit of space on my side of the small desk, but who cared? The iMac G3 was the hottest new computer available. After an hour or so of assembly and cleanup, it was ready to power on. I plugged in the ethernet cable but decided to call my mom before connecting to the internet. My transparent, unisonic phone lit up and rang before I could dial.

"Hello," I answered, twirling the coiled cord around my index finger.

"Hello, Jellybean," my mom said excitedly. "Did you get it?"

"I did! I was just about to call you. Thank you so much. I love it!"

"Oh good, honey! I'm so glad. How are classes going?"

"Fine. Boring. I was just about to study for a test. How's Dad?"

"He's doing okay. He's having his moments where he forgets stuff, but he's doing better. Are you coming to visit for Halloween Break?"

"Yeah! The student council voted on it. We're swapping Spring Break for Halloween Break. *Most* of the campus is excited about it. Oh! And ask the nurses to give him crossword puzzles in the morning."

"Oh, okay. Well, get back to homework. I can't wait to see you, Jellybean. I'll see you then. Love you."

"Love you too, Mom."

I took the note from the box and stuck it to the bottom of my monitor. The internet took far too long to connect. Static, followed by pinging noises, filled the room while I lit a candle and some incense. The flame flickered as the heavily scented smoke twisted over it.

I moved the window's makeshift curtain to the side; it was just a cheap blanket with a funky, colorful pattern and a peace sign printed on it, but it functioned the same. It was dark outside, and students trekked through the grass to some frat party.

Besides the fact that it was past my usual bedtime, I had no interest in parties. I loved sleep. Maybe too much, even. But the internet finally connected, and I was too eager to go to bed. I sat in my chair and opened the browser excitedly. It was slow, so I made a note to look into broadband and stuck it on my monitor next to the note from my mom.

I opened my email, only to be disappointed by spam. I spotted one from my great aunt Genie and clicked on it. Chain mail.

> THIS MESSAGE IS BAD LUCK!
> SEND THIS MESSAGE TO 10 FRIENDS, OR
> YOU WILL HAVE BAD LUCK FOREVER!!!!

I rolled my eyes, closing out of it. I opened another email from my best friend, Harvey.

> PUFF, PUFF, PASS
> YOU'VE JUST BEEN PASSED THE BLUNT.
> PASS THIS BLUNT TO 4 FRIENDS TO KEEP
> THE GREEN IN ROTATION. DON'T BE GREEDY
> WITH THAT SHIT, OR YOU'LL ONLY GET
> SEEDS FOR A YEAR.

I laughed. If I was going to get chain mail, at least it could be amusing instead of the same old superstitious garbage that ended in a threat if I didn't forward it to everyone in my contacts.

Harvey was the only true friend I had on campus. He was an unlikely companion; he played on the football team and had a perfect body with a honey-roasted tan and bright blue eyes. His frosted tip highlights were never brassy, and even his eyebrows were perfectly groomed. Best of all, unlike a lot of guys, he never made a move on me.

Harvey never dated. He didn't enjoy hanging out with his teammates, going to parties, or drinking. Maybe that's why we both got along so well. Neither of us had any interest in most of the social norms of college life in this year of our lord, Snoop Dogg, 1998. I felt safe with him.

The door busted open, and Neveah and her two minions stumbled in, laughing. I rolled my eyes and checked the time, surprised to see her back already.

"Wow. New record for Tommy. What was it, forty seconds this time?" I jabbed.

She sucked her teeth and turned to me. "Sick! You got one of those new computers? In blue? So Cute. Can I use it?"

"No. And you can't use my *bed* either."

"Okay, like, I said I was sorry. We were a little high."

"Whatever."

Neveah was gorgeous, popular, and a bit oblivious when it came to manners or personal boundaries. She was used to getting whatever she wanted, and it made living with her less than fun. She and her clique came and went at all hours, barging in or letting the door slam shut on their way out. She wasn't the worst, though, so I decided to deal with the evil I knew rather than risk changing roommates and ending up with a band geek who played tuba at 7:00 AM.

Neveah set a wooden box on her side of the desk. I would never expect her to bring home something like it, but as autumn descended, "spooky" became every girl's aesthetic, I supposed. The box was old and weathered but solid and crafted well. She lifted a decorative silver latch and opened it. It was lined with vibrant black velvet, and I couldn't help but notice what was inside.

"A *Ouija board*? Really?"

One of her friends walked over to the desk and grabbed it. "Yeah. We found it at an estate sale. Creepy old place, but that's what I get for hanging out with white chicks," Brandy said as she lifted the board out with soft, dark-brown hands. "Wanna play?"

"No. I'm good. Say hi to Satan for me, though," I quipped.

She rolled her almond-shaped eyes and set the board down on the desk with a soft clunk, a testament to how heavy it was. I couldn't take my eyes off of it. It was made of ivory with elaborate carvings of moon phases and beach morning glories flowers stained in a soft, splotchy indigo. The curling letters and a deep crack on one side were filled with polished sterling silver.

Brandy took out the mouse, or whatever it was called. It was also made of ivory and was triangular with rounded corners. The carvings etched into it were just as intricate, and the hollow window was filled with clear crystal glass. There were divots on the sides as if it had been worn down from years of fingers pressing onto its surface.

As authentically demonic as it was, it was stunning. Neveah, with her butterfly clips and Britney posters, could never appreciate such a treasure, and I pitied its last owner.

Brandy and Skyler sat on the edge of the bed to press their fingers on the mouse, and Neveah pulled up a chair next to me and held the other side of the ivory triangle.

"Oh, wait, turn out the lights!" Skyler exclaimed, her freckled skin just as white as the board. I rolled my eyes as Neveah hopped up and flipped the switch. When she returned, she gave me a sideways glance. The glow of my computer was apparently a nuisance, so I turned the screen away from their silly game, lowered the brightness, and opened another email. I had received yet another chain letter.

"Well, luckily, we already have a candle going. Let's see. What should we ask first?" Neveah asked, rolling her shoulders cheerfully.

They giggled and greeted the fake spirits as I clicked through my emails, rolling my eyes.

"So stupid," I muttered under my breath.

"Okay! I got it. Will I pass my algebra class?" Skyler inquired. They giggled as the mouse moved. It landed over the "NO" etched in fancy letters. "Well, why not?" she whined.

"Wait, wait! It's spelling something. Are you moving it? I'm not moving it, I swear," Brandi said excitedly.

"I'm not moving it either! O. M. G," Neveah squealed.

"W. H. O. R. E," they spelled out together. Skyler's mouth dropped open. Her bright blue eyes rolled, and she folded her thin arms over her chest.

"You guys suck."

"Blame Brandi. I wasn't moving it," Neveah barked.

"Girl, you're buggin'. I wasn't moving that thing!"

I huffed, rolling my eyes again. They were *all* buggin'.

I shivered. The room was chillier than usual. I never minded the cold but curled up in my computer chair anyway and rubbed my arms. My eyes shot toward the Post-it notes on my monitor. I swore I saw them in my periphery, flapping in a breeze.

"Let's try again," Neveah said. "Who here do you want to fuck tonight?"

They burst into a fit of laughter, but the noise quieted to giggles as the mouse glided.

"J. E—" they began spelling in unison.

"That's working well, isn't it? No one here has a name starting with 'J,'" I comment, exiting my email and pulling my textbook into my lap. The computer screen lit the page softly.

"L. L. Y. B."

I wasn't listening to the letters at that point, trying extra hard to block them out and flipping to the end-of-chapter questions.

"E. A. N?"

"*Jellybean?*" Neveah asked, confused.

I glanced up from my book, a clear absence of humor masking my face.

"Very funny. Not convinced. You saw the note from my mom on the computer box."

"What?" Neveah shook her head and focused back on the board. "Whatever. When will Tommy tell me he loves me?"

I rolled my eyes. Finally, the board was silent for a long moment. I studied a question, rubbing the goosebumps on my arm. The hairs stuck straight up as if pulling to a static charge. The air tasted metallic. I licked my lips, reading.

What part of the brain do adolescents primarily use since their frontal lobe is not fully developed, resulting in impulsive behavior?

I knew this one but couldn't remember. I closed my eyes, tapping my pencil on the page. A chill ran up my spine again, and I grabbed a throw blanket from my bed and wrapped it around my shoulders. I looked back down at the question.

"Um, hello? *Ouija demon!* When will Tommy tell me he loves me?" Neveah asked again, more urgently. *God, her voice is annoying. Focus.*

I chewed my lip and read the question under my breath.

"What part of the brain do adolescents primarily use since their frontal lobe is not fully developed, resulting in impulsive behavior?" I whispered. A breeze lifted the corner of the page, and I looked up, wondering if one of the girls was trying to annoy me more than usual. But they were all focused on their dumb game.

Maybe it was the air conditioner kicking on. Something was causing a breeze.

"Ohh! It's moving!" Skyler squealed.

They spelled out whatever lame answer they wanted to hear about fuck-boy Tommy. I didn't love Neveah, but I wasn't unkind enough to break it to her that Tommy just wanted to get laid. He was never going to say it. They got quiet.

"Who the hell is *Amy G Dala?*" Brandy demanded.

A shiver ran up my spine, and I sat up straighter.

"What?" I asked them.

"That's what it spelled, right?" She looked at the other two for confirmation. "Oh my gosh! Doesn't that cheerleader, Amy, have a thing for Tommy?"

Neveah's face turned green.

"As if!" she squealed.

"No... What were the letters?" I asked. The three looked over at me, annoyed.

"A.M.Y.G.D.A.L.A," Skyler stated plainly as she glanced down at the notebook where she had recorded the Ouija's answers.

"*Amygdala?*" I repeated in a cautious tone, goosebumps rising all over my body again.

"What's that supposed to mean?"

"It's the part of the brain that adolescents primarily use when their frontal lobe hasn't developed enough yet... resulting in... impulsive behavior," I answered, totally weirded out.

"As if, *squared*, Buffy. Like *amygdala?* Why would a Ouija demon want to tell us that?" Neveah laughed.

"Ah!" Skyler shrieked. "It's moving!"

Neveah hurried back to the board and placed her square-tip

French manicured nails on the mouse as it moved. They read silently this time. As I watched, my computer screen went dark, defaulting to the black screensaver. I paid no attention to it, focusing on the triangle moving in the scant light.

The flickering candlelight caused the crystal window to sparkle as it glided. The smoke from the incense hovered over their heads, gathering into a cloud. For a moment, I thought it took the shape of a face. I blinked my tired eyes.

It was as if an invisible man was hovering over them, his head haloed by the scented smoke. I saw an arm reaching out toward me. My heart pounded, and I froze. My jaw was clenched painfully shut, and I blinked again. When I opened my eyes, the smoke was dancing upward without a trace of human features. My muscles relaxed, and my mouth went slack.

"*For her?*" Brandy asked. "For who? Who is '*her?*'"

I stood slowly, setting the book down on my bed. Cautiously, I walked over to them, standing behind Neveah to look at the mouse sliding across the magnificent board. The silver letters magnified and sparkled as the crystal window hovered over them. My chest rose and fell fast as the word was spelled out.

Jellybean.

The candle went out, and the room fell into pitch black. All of us screamed. I scrambled across the room in search of the light switch. Feeling my way through the darkness, my hands trembled. All three of them were yelling, demanding that I turn the light on. I could hardly hear them with my heart pounding in my ears. I found the wall and patted it, trying to feel anything familiar that would guide me to the switch.

A chilled hand ran from my exposed midriff to my navel, pulling me backward roughly. My back hit a cold, firm body. An eager breath brushed against my ear just before a deep, raspy growl rumbled against it. I let out a high-pitched scream that burned my throat. Jumping, I finally found the switch and flipped it on.

Light washed over the dorm, and the hand released me instantly. I spun quickly to find all three girls still on the other side of the room, hands over their mouths. Suddenly, they broke into fits of laughter, Brandi falling backward onto the bed and grabbing her belly. But my face was drained of blood, and every part of my body was shaking. I rubbed my palm over where the hand was. It had been freezing, and the nerves in my skin still hummed with the remnants of the sensation. I swallowed hard.

Skyler struck a Zippo lighter with her thumb and lit the candle again. "Okay, got it. You can turn the light back off, Buffy."

"No. I think you guys need to put that thing away now. Seriously."

"Oh, *now* you're spooked?" Brandy teased. "It's all in fun. Let's find out its name, shall we?"

"Guys..."

But they didn't listen. Brandi walked over to me, reaching past my shoulder and flipping off the light. She winked.

"It's all good, girl. It's just a game," she said before skipping back and landing on the bed with a bounce that made her wavy micro braids sway over her back. They pressed their fingers into the mouse again, giggling. I warmed my shoulders and walked toward them as unease shifted the food in my stomach.

"Hey, Ouija demon, what is your name?" Neveah asked flirtatiously.

"B. A—" They read together.

"Guys, stop it." My heart was pounding. Hearing the name of an entity that just grabbed me sounded like a terrible idea.

"...N. E."

"*Bane?*" I whispered.

"That's kind of hot," Skyler giggled. A cold wind wrapped around me, hardening my nipples. I drew in a shallow breath, tensing, and I thought I heard a groan.

"That's enough," I blurted, charging toward them. I snatched the mouse and carelessly tossed it aside. It tumbled and bounced over my keyboard. The sparkling window magnified the M key. Then I seized the *Ouija* board. It was heavier than I expected, and its coldness pricked my fingers.

Neveah grabbed my arm. "Hey! What are you doing? That's mine!"

"I don't care. It's creeping me out." I pulled my arm from her hold, put the board in its box, and closed it.

"Well, don't you feel crunchy, ms. *skepticism?*" Brandi teased, rolling her neck.

"No. I feel like it's late. I need to get to sleep, and Amy is going to be at the party that Tommy's fraternity is throwing, so—"

"Oh, hell no!" Neveah jumped up and grabbed her purse. She misted her entire body in a tornado of Lovespell body spray, making me cough and waft it away. "Let's bounce, guys."

In no time, they were rushing out the door. I sat in my computer chair in silence. The flickering candle was the only source of light. I preferred it dim; it was usually calming. But strangely, I didn't feel alone. Fear simmered under the surface as heat prickled my cheeks. I shook my head. It was nothing. I was paranoid from their creepy little game. They were messing with me. They had to have been.

I clicked my computer mouse, and the screen came to life.

"Let me guess, more *chain mail*. Okay, I'll bite," I said out loud, trying to break the creeping silence in the room. I read the email animatedly.

> "DESTINY IS CALLING!
> SEND THIS EMAIL TO:
> 0 FRIENDS AND YOU'LL NEVER FIND TRUE LOVE
> 5 FRIENDS AND A MYSTERIOUS MAN WILL PURSUE YOU
> 10 FRIENDS AND YOU'LL GET THAT PLUS A NEW CELL PHONE!"

I laughed.

"Phhh... Okay, but I do want a cell phone."

I went to forward it, knowing very well it was silly nonsense. When I went to type in Harvey's address, I noticed the Ouija board mouse still on my keyboard and froze. The window magnified the number two.

"Two?" I clearly remembered it being over the M. *Or I thought so...* I grabbed the mouse. As soon as my fingers touched it, I shivered. It was ice cold. My computer screen flickered, and I swore I felt it gliding seamlessly over the bumpy keys. My body stiffened, jaw clenched tight and muscles rigid. Fear flooded my blood as the ivory dragged my hand with it, spelling something. It moved to five letters, looping and gliding before coming to a stop.

"*Sleep.*"

I gasped. My body was freed from its immobile state, and I lifted my hand quickly to hug my fist against my turbulent chest. Before I had time to think about it, I grabbed the keyboard and threw it, causing the Ouija mouse to fly to the other side of the desk and tumble to the ground. My keyboard, hanging by its cord, swayed against the side of the desk. I shook my head and huffed out an exasperated laugh.

No. Ghosts and demons aren't real. I reeled the keyboard back in by its cord. In denial, I shoved down the fear and acted like everything was normal, forwarding the email to ten friends.

But the feeling of someone's presence behind me, next to me, or looming over me never left. After trying to focus on anything but that *and failing,* I gave up. The monitor slept.

I needed more than a splash of water on my face to get out of this superstitious mindset. So, I laid out some sleeping clothes, grabbed a towel, and went to the community bathroom to wash up. My mind was playing tricks on me, and a shower was the remedy. Afterward, I would come back and indulge in my favorite pastime: *sleep.*

3

BANE

I stood by the door, my eyes following her wherever she went. I would leave her alone momentarily and let her convince herself it was all in her head. She would feel silly for thinking anything of the small tricks I played to haunt and seduce her. I would torment her little by little, making her question her sanity. Then, I would torment her more until she broke.

I waited for this haunting my entire life and had never felt a rush quite like terrifying her. *Buffy*. Her fear was unique. It was made for me. If I were not careful, she would bring me to my knees before I could bend her to my will. I wondered what she sounded like when she cried and what her tears tasted like on her cheek. I craved her fear, but she was making me work for it. It was impossible to walk away from.

Wrapped in a towel, she walked through me and reached for the door. My eyes skated down her shoulder blades, and she paused. She felt me, that staticky cold just inches from her back. She did not react with fear. She was analyzing the feeling, squinting her eyes. I admired how skeptical she was. It would do her no good, though. She was *mine*. She would be *mine* forever. When I was through with her, she would never wake up in this world again.

I inched closer to her back, watching the tiny hairs on her neck stand up and reach toward me. She took a slow, deep breath, straightening her back. Her breath clouded just beyond her lips, and her skin tightened as the feeling of dread crept up her spine. But she barely even flinched. I smirked, bringing my fangs close to her soft neck. *She is a fighter*.

I grabbed a swatch of her hair, lifting it to my nose and smelling it. Orange blossoms and sweet, fresh sweat. She spun around, but I held a strand tight, ripping it from her scalp. She cupped her skull and gasped.

"Sss. Ow..."

We were face-to-face, and yet her eyes searched the room beyond me. Buffy scratched lightly at her scalp. I looked down at her, cocking my head to the side and glaring at her pouty lips. Then she shook her head and huffed. Turning back to the door, she grabbed the handle and swung it open to leave the room, tense but strong. She *thought* she was strong, at least. I would put that to the test. I could not wait to break her. She would never question my love for her then.

I stepped forward to follow her to the showers but could not pass the threshold. Bound by the board's magic, I jolted at the doorway and stumbled back. I growled as the door slowly swung shut, and her petite frame disappeared around the corner.

Angry, I turned for the box on her friend's bed. My hands went through it as I tried to pick it up. It slipped through my fingers again like a ghost. I could not move the Ouija board and take it to her any more than I could smash it on the ground in anger. It was the one thing in the room I could not touch. Of course, I knew I could not manipulate my invitation to their space, but Buffy made it hard to think clearly.

I would have to wait until she was close enough to the board to haunt her. But if I scared her too well before she was marked, she might not come back. I ground my teeth.

This is going to be a problem. I could not let Buffy have any means of escape. I needed to have her in my reach at all times. She was *mine*. I pondered the possibility of coming back via the Sacred Sands, but that had its limits, too, draining my power with every touch. I knew once I started touching her, I would not be able to stop, and that would exhaust my energy. If she were this much of a fighter already, it would be too risky, and I wouldn't be able to fuck her properly.

There had to be another way. I looked around the room, fiddling through her belongings as I thought of ways to haunt her. I scratched my claw along her desk. I could bring her to the Dream World, but she could not stay long and would have to remain on the shore. That would help me get my cocks wet tonight, but haunting her into submission until the night of her marking was another story. I had to haunt her in the human world, too.

I traced her bite marks on the surface of a pencil. Her cursive was scrolled along a notebook underneath it. The script was perfectly timeless and classic, like an old spell. A thought crossed my mind. *If she summoned me here through a spell, that could solve my problem.* But it could not be only her. It took entire covens to raise a demon to its full potential and give them enough domain. How could I get enough humans to summon me here through a spell and give me unrestricted ability to move, appear, and *touch*?

I flicked the pencil lightly. It rolled across the desk and hit the letter-encrusted board plugged into the blue box. I looked at it for a long moment. Smiling, I shifted my eyes to the blue, glowing machine it was plugged into. My little dream had shown me a clever trick.

"*Chain mail...*" I said, repeating the term she had uttered under her breath.

I traced my hands along the board of letters. It was the same concept as a Ouija. The only difference was that the blue box recorded my message, and I could send it to anyone. I typed in my commands and did as she had, addressing the mail to the "contacts," including her. The more people that opened this, the more they would send it to. The more people who read it, the stronger the spell. I needed her to say it above anyone else, and I would make sure she did. I hit send and smiled wryly. Now, it was a matter of her opening it.

She was taking too long, and I was growing impatient. I rubbed my hand along her pillow and mattress. There was a dip in the bed where her petite body had laid. I could read a bed like a palm, and it was clear that my little dream loved to sleep. *Of course, she does; she's mine.* I could tell she went to bed early, slept in late when she could, and was difficult to wake. My spirited cock coiled excitedly. *Fuck, I love a sleepy girl.*

I grew hard, wondering what she was doing in the shower that was taking so long. After grabbing a fistful of the clothes she had piled next to her laundry basket, I pressed them against my face, smelling her scent. I found a pair of lace underwear and dragged my long, forked tongue along the crotch. I tasted the faintest flavor of her cum, and my eyes rolled back.

"*Oh fuck,*" I growled, needing to taste it fresh from her. I could not calm myself, waiting for her to return to the room. I sat on the floor and rubbed the panties over my length.

Finally, the doorknob turned. I squeezed her panties in my hand until they disappeared, and barely lifted my head as I glared at her from under my brow. There was a vicious need burning in my soul. The smell of shampoo and soap wafted over me as she walked past. Then, she dropped her towel, and my heart raced as her damp skin glistened in the flickering candlelight. I stood quickly and walked behind her, my chest a breath away from her back.

She moved the towel over her body, spreading her legs to pat herself dry. My chest heaved. I wanted to drag my claws down her back and lick the blood from her skin. I wanted to pin her down and fuck her. I needed to see her eyes full of terror. I needed to hear her scream and cry as I came for her. I needed to drag her to the Dream World. There, she could scream. She could cry as loud as she wanted. No one would hear her. My little dream, my perfect Buffy. I would worship her with my fiercest terror.

She raised her arms to put on a shirt, and her perfect tits tightened in the chill of my presence. She tensed, swallowing hard. Buffy was questioning what that nagging feeling was. She was just nervous, but it felt *incredible*.

Fucking tease.

She bent over to step into a lacy, black thong, and I fell to my knees, my face inches from her beautiful pussy. I came undone. It was so small and wet. Her asshole looked so sweet and tight. I wanted to tear her apart. My breath against her exposed center caused goosebumps to race up her back. Buffy shivered theatrically, snapping her spine straight as she stood. I sat kneeling behind her in awe as she shivered in sweet fear. *She will be the death of me.*

She struck a lighter against a small glass pipe, sucking on one end. Crawling into bed on her knees, she blew the smoke out with her head tilted back and released a hoarse cough. She placed the pipe on her desk and plopped into the mattress. She lay on her belly, hugged a pillow, and took a soothing breath. She loved being in bed, nuzzling into the sheets and releasing the tension in her body. She was relaxed and calm.

I floated over her, watching her body sink into comfort. She was so fucking perfect. Her breathing slowed, her body going limp as she fell into REM sleep. I filled my fist with her soft hair and leaned in close to her ear, breathing in her scent.

"Are you ready, my little dream?"

4

BUFFY

I was at the beach in the middle of the night. The sand appeared to be made of diamond dust, twinkling as my toes pressed into it. Vines of purple beach morning glories crawled down the sand toward the waterline, blooming in the light of a crystal moon. The indigo sea boiled in different spots, steam swirling to the black, star-studded sky. The rest of the water was turbulent, peaking like mountain tops that rose four feet high or more. But no waves crashed on the shore; there was just a seamless transition from dark ocean to white sand.

I stared at the glowing silver clouds that moved across the sky. I felt a sense of déjà vu that I dreamed of this place before but couldn't remember. This felt more vivid than a dream.

I couldn't move again, and fear knotted my stomach as I felt the same presence that was in my dorm. I tried to run, but my legs wouldn't respond. My body suddenly levitated, turning horizontal. Trying to remain calm, I slowly floated down to the shimmering sand. My heart pounded, and my breath failed to slow.

I strained to sit up or grab at the earth. I tried to speak, but my jaw was locked shut, clenching so tight I swore my teeth would shatter. A cold breeze passed over me, and my white nightgown blew right off. Naked on the beach and paralyzed, I wanted to guard my body from being seen, but I lay utterly exposed on the shimmering shore.

"Buffy," a gravelly voice, deep and indulgent, murmured in my ear. I shrieked with a hollow gasp, eyes wide and searching. A chilled breath on my collarbone made the hairs on my neck stand up. Panic flooded my veins. A tear fell from my eye as I remembered that I couldn't scream or fight. "Finally."

A cold palm glided down my collarbone and across my chest. I was too afraid to look down and see it, so I squinted my eyes shut and sobbed. I couldn't even guard my body from his touch. His hand passed over my nipple, and my face flushed with embarrassment. It stopped under the other breast, held my side tightly, and pulled me down.

My body sank into the sand slowly. Frightened that I wouldn't be able to breathe soon, I tried to thrash, but I could only make small jerks. I screamed through clenched teeth. As I sank, another hand caressed my waist and lowered to my hip. It brushed over my clit and lips as it moved to grip my inner thigh. He pulled my leg open, and fear flooded my veins again.

I tried to move with all of my strength, but my mind still could not command my body past useless shuddering. His breathing became excited. In a panic, I fought hard as the sand inched closer to my eyes. He was pulling me down into the cold, shimmering earth, burying me alive as he touched me.

His hard, chilled body pressed against my back as he hissed and groaned excitedly in my ear. Something large and heavy pushed against my thigh, flexing until it brushed against my entrance. I yelped and managed to writhe for a moment.

"Sss. That's it, my little dream. Are you ready for me?" he asked in a tone meant for lovers. The tip rubbed against my entrance hard, and my moisture soaked it. His grasp on my thigh tightened as he pulled me open wider.

My jaw unfroze. I yelled as loud as I could, but my voice seemed to fall flat.

"Help!" I screamed as he pulled me underground. But my pleading words came out in a hoarse whisper. "Help!" I could barely move my arms. "Sto—" Sand trickled into my mouth, and I slammed my lips shut, screaming from my throat. Tears fell from my eyes as I panicked. "Stop... Please!" I sobbed through tight lips.

A long growl filled my ears as his hold became painful. He thrust his hips hard, and my slick lips parted, but not enough for him to penetrate. He pushed again, harder.

A loud noise crashed through the space. The hands fell away. The sand fell away. And even though my eyes could see the sky above me, I opened them again. This time, I was looking at my dark dorm room ceiling. Neveah was stumbling in, cackling, and wasted. I shot up, panting.

My body was trembling violently, and tears streaked down my face as I remembered the growling. I could still hear it echoing in my ears, like the T-Rex from Jurassic Park. I wiped the back of my wrist across my cheeks and looked myself over. I was still wearing my oversized Nirvana t-shirt and black lace thong, the latter of which was soaked and pulled to the side. A clear, silverish fluid was smeared on my thigh. I wiped it off frantically. When I looked at my alarm clock, it flashed 2:04 AM.

"Girl, you missed it! That party was the *bomb*!"

I rubbed my eyes. "Neveah! What the hell, dude? Can you be quiet for once? I was sleeping!" I yelled with a shaky voice, more out of terror and confusion than actually being mad. Barging in late at night was a regular occurrence for her. I was used to it by now. And truthfully, I was thankful to be woken up this time, something I never thought I would say. But Neveah was as cluelessly inconsiderate as she was bubbly, so I refused to feel bad about my outburst.

"I'm sorry, okay! Hey, can I check my email really quick?" she asked, throwing herself in my small swivel chair and bringing my screen to life. I squinted, the light burning my eyes.

"It's two in the morning, dude. No! Jesus. I hate living with you sometimes!"

"Wow. Way to kill my vibe. I'll be quick, and then you can go back to being a grandma."

Fully awake, I sat up in bed; the posters covering my wall crinkled as my back pressed into them. I reached behind the computer monitor and grabbed my pipe, packing a small bowl of crippy. Harvey always got me the best pot. It was stinky and sticky, with purple fuzzy hairs springing out of it.

Neveah clicked away on my keyboard as I struck the lighter and took a hit. I held it in for a long moment, hoping I would be able to get back to sleep and not have another terrifying nightmare. My heart rate slowed, and I relaxed as the skunky smoke filled my lungs. I blew it out, the smoke looking blue from the monitor's glow. But inches in front of me, the smoke took the shape of a face. It was a man with a square jaw and deep-set eyes. Startled, I waved my hand through it quickly, batting away the image. I tensed, bringing my knees to my chest. *Why did it look so familiar?*

"You okay, Buff?"

"I'm fine. Bad batch of weed, I think." I put the pipe on the desk and laid down, pulling the covers over me.

"Really, dude? You sent me chain mail? I can't stand those."

"And I can't stand being woken up at two AM or having a roommate with no respect for boundaries," I groused, pulling the blanket over my head and landing on my side as I turned away from the bright screen.

"Some people never grew up with siblings, and it shows. *Delete.* Actually, you know what? *Forward.* Why not? I don't need a mysterious man, but I'd *love* a new cell phone."

"Are you done?" I snapped, lowering the blanket under my chin.

"Hold on, damn."

I stared at the wall. It felt like I was lying next to someone. I pulled an extra pillow under the covers to my chest and nestled into it. I imagined I did have someone there, someone nice. I wrapped my leg around the long pillow, tightening my hold. I remembered the hand on my inner thigh in my dream and smirked. Terrifying experience aside, the thought of my legs getting pulled apart and being taken left me warm and restless. *If only it could happen when I'm not being haunted by a demon*, I joked internally.

"Oh, hey, you got an email from an unknown sender. Is a mysterious man pursuing *you?*"

"Doubt it. Unless a sleep paralysis demon has taken a recent interest in me 'cus my bitch roommate decided to fuck with a haunted Ouija board."

"Wow, this one is pretty fucked."

"Neveah, I know you're not checking my emails right now," I said with my lips pressed into the pillow. If this pillow *were* the perfect man, he'd find a way to get my roommate to stay out of my shit. The high was in full effect, and I nuzzled back into the imaginary man. My mind was convinced he was brushing hair from my face with icy fingers and pulling me against him by my ass. I could almost feel it. *Not a bad batch of weed, after all.* I smiled softly.

"No, seriously, who sends shit like this? 'Send this spell to three friends, and sleep naked, or never sleep again and die for me.'"

"What?" I said, furrowing my brows. Chain mail could get pretty wack, but this was another level of dark and oddly specific to the one thing I'd cave for—my sleep. I couldn't imagine a worse way to die than sleep deprivation.

> "READ IT OUT LOUD:
> RISE, RISE, DEMON OF SLEEP.
> THE MOON KING COMES TO TAKE HIS QUEEN.
> SPIRIT TO BONE, GHOST TO FLESH.
> HE CLAIMS HIS BRIDE.
> NEVER WAKE AGAIN."

My hold on the pillow got tighter. The blood drained from my face. I turned to her slowly. "Who sent that?" I asked with a weak voice.

"I told you. It says, 'unknown sender.'"

"Neveah, I don't know what kind of sick games you're playing lately, but it's not funny anymore."

"What did I do?"

I sat up, pushing the swivel chair away from my computer to her side of the dorm. "The Ouija board. *Jellybean?* My mother calls me that, and you know it. And guessing the answers to my A&P homework? How the hell do you even know what an amygdala is? You major in business!"

"You're right. That is a bad batch of pot. You're totally buggin'." She picked up the Ouija mouse from the floor. "Is this what you're so paranoid about? It's just a silly game, Buffy. Chillax. Watch, I'll send the demon away."

"Send yourself away, and take that thing with you. Lose it. It's freaking haunted or something."

She pulled the board out and put the mouse on top, smiling smugly. "Oh, *Bane*," she sang seductively. "Are you here, you big demonic hunk?"

A wind passed by. I sprung from my bed, brushing my shoulder off like I stepped through a spider's web.

"Neveah, you need to stop. For real!" I demanded.

"Oh... my..." she whispered under her breath. Her face was gaunt and focused on the board beneath her fingers. "He says he wants to fuck you in the ass!" she shrieked in fake surprise and then busted out in a fit of laughter. I walked over to her and tried to grab the mouse. She held it out of reach. "Oh, come on. You really think this is real?"

"All I know is creepy shit has been happening ever since you guys used it. I'm having wack-ass dreams, and I swear someone keeps *touching* me." My shoulders tensed as I motioned my open hand over my torso frantically.

"Well, then maybe you should find out what he wants. Make sure he isn't going to kill you and screw your dead body in a ritual or something." She gave a drunken smile, nodding to the board.

"I will do anything if you promise to be quiet so I can sleep."

She nodded again. I sat across from her, the board between us.

She set the mouse on it, grabbed my hand, and guided it to the ivory triangle. Its frigid surface instantly made me uneasy, and the air again filled with a metallic scent.

"Go ahead. If you *really* think you're being haunted, you better find out why."

I huffed. Neveah waited with our fingers on the edge of the mouse. I glanced at her, knowing she would think I was ridiculous for talking to a spirit. I tried anyway.

"Were you in my dream?"

It moved quickly to 'YES.' I glared at Neveah, wondering if she was nudging it along.

I hesitated for a moment before asking, "What do you want?"

It moved over the letters, and I watched in confusion.

Forward it.

I shrunk back and rolled my eyes.

"This is stupid. What demon wants me to forward an email, Neveah? You could be a little more creative."

"I'm not moving it, loser," she said, flicking my arm hard.

"Ow!" I yelped, cupping the sore spot.

Immediately, Neveah swayed and grabbed her own arm.

"Oh god. Fucking Juger bombs got me fucked up." She burped sour and wet. "I think I felt that flick for you."

"Serves you right."

"I didn't move the damn mouse. Ask it something I wouldn't know. Watch."

"No, I'm good."

"Bane, what did she dream about?"

I looked at her, tired, high, and over her games. She was proving herself wrong for me. How drunk do you have to be to ask something you'd never know the answer to? The mouse moved, the crystal hovering over one letter at a time. It seemed to move forever, and Neveah jotted down the letters on a notebook, keeping one hand on the mouse. I yawned and rubbed my eyes with my free palm.

"He says, 'into the sand.' Does that make sense?"

My body ran cold. My heart fell into my stomach. I tried my hardest to stay calm. This had to be a joke. But there is no way Neveah could have made that up. Just in case I wasn't having a bad high, I proceeded with caution. As terrified as I was, I had to engage with the demon and find out what kind of danger I was in. After a few measured breaths, I spoke to Bane in earnest for the first time.

"Why did you bring me there?"

It moved instantly, and I held my breath as he answered.

To take you.

I didn't know what that meant. Take me where? For how long? To do what?

"Why...?" was all I could manage.

To mark you.

I shook my head, glancing up at Neveah. Pulling my hand away from the mouse, I sighed. "I just want to know if this thing is going to kill me, and he's being cryptic as hell."

Neveah raised her over-plucked eyebrows like I was being weird and making the whole thing up. Then she flinched and drew her hand back.

"Shit! I think it moved," she shrieked.

I touched it, my blue and silver crackle nail polish shimmering in the glow of my monitor. She followed suit, and it glided to speak to me.

Sleep.

I withdrew my hand, scowling at my roommate, then stood up and backed away. Shaking my head, I crawled into my warm bed and held the pillow under the covers.

"Get rid of it in the morning."

"You're not going to forward the email? Really. At least sleep naked." Neveah put the board away and stripped down. "Shit. I will."

She forwarded the email and powered down the computer. As she crawled into bed in the pitch-black room, I lay wide awake. She was asleep in no time, snoring lightly and not moving an inch. I couldn't, though. I was terrified to close my eyes, to sink into the sand again.

I didn't sleep at all that night. My eyes felt like they were going to bleed, dried up, and bulging out of my skull. Neveah, on the other hand, slept naked in the hopes she could get some demon dick. Unfortunately, Bane didn't seem interested in pursuing her instead.

I watched the clock tick slowly until seven AM. The sunlight bled through the window, stinging my retinas. Neveah started to stir, groaning painfully before hissing and waking fully.

"Fuck!" she yelled, sitting up. "What the hell happened to my arm?"

Startled by her emergent cries, I ran over to her. I gasped. Her arm was black and blue and swollen.

"Oh my God, Neveah! Can you move it?"

She tried and sobbed, "No. I think it's broken."

"That's crazy, I saw you last night. It was fine. You were moving it fine!" I panicked as she stood up. She tried to move it again and hollered in pain as it practically dangled. "You flicked me with that arm! It was fine last night."

"Well, it's fucked now!"

"Okay, okay. Let me help you get dressed. I'll take you to the clinic." She sobbed as I helped her into a shirt, pulling it over her head and guiding her mangled arm through the right hole. "Let's get you to the nurse."

5
BUFFY

I hadn't slept in three days. That first night, I was too wigged out to fall asleep. But returning to the reality of everyday life snapped me out of it, and I felt silly for letting the darkness get to me like a child. I sketched the face I had seen onto my notebook, and I could swear I dreamed of that face before. But the only thing I was certain of was that I needed a good night's sleep.

After self-medicating with a bowl or two, I attempted to squeeze my eyes shut and relax the next night. But I couldn't fall asleep, no matter how hard I tried. The third night I took warm showers and wore my coziest oversized t-shirts and fuzzy knee-high socks. None of it worked. I had never experienced insomnia before, and it was driving me mad.

After three sleepless nights and three days of fighting to focus in class, dragging my tired legs, and forgetting simple things, I was getting desperate. Neveah hadn't gotten rid of the board. She kept it out of my sight and didn't use it again, but insisted it was too priceless to throw away. She brushed off my exhausted pleas, telling me I was being stupid. It made it hard to feel bad that her arm had been mysteriously broken. She didn't know how it happened, but I had my suspicions.

It was night four. Neveah slept over at Tommy's but somehow found time to taunt me by leaving beach morning glories on my pillow again. Our university was over thirty minutes from the nearest beach. *How is she getting these every day when we are this far inland?* They smelled nice, so I didn't grill her about it. If she wanted to go through the trouble to tease me about the board, this was the most benign way she could. And as pathetic as it sounded, I had never gotten flowers before. Even though it was with malice, I enjoyed them. I lifted the petals to my nose as I took in their scent before exchanging them with the dead ones in a mason jar of water on my windowsill.

It was quiet, and I was free of distractions. Still, I sat at my desk, looking at a diagram of the heart and not registering any part of it. My colored pencils and pen sat unused. Sleep-deprived, my brain just wouldn't work anymore. A tear stung my eyes for no reason at all. Lack of sleep had a way of making one overly emotional. Finally, I shoved the diagram away for later.

It was nearly two AM. More tears stung my eyes at the thought of another sleepless night. I checked my email before trying to sleep. 'Unknown sender' emailed me again, and goosebumps raced along my body. It was the same chain mail message he sent me every night since Neveah first found it in my inbox. It demanded I sleep naked, or I'd never sleep again, with some wack-ass spell that I refused to read out loud.

Could it be that simple? I wondered as I stared at the words. Just one night of slumber was all I needed. Maybe I *was* imagining the whole thing. I hadn't been haunted in days aside from a staticky, cold presence and an occasional pull at my nipples that I was sure was all in my head. Maybe it *was* a bad batch of pot that night. But also, maybe if I tried this silly spell thing and slept naked, my mind would trick itself into allowing me to sleep. With a glance at my unfinished homework hanging out of its folder, I sighed and gave in. What harm could it do to try? I took the board out from under Neveah's bed, held the mouse against my lips so the imaginary demon could hear me loud and clear, and groaned his creepy spell into its crystal window unenthusiastically.

"*Rise, rise, demon of sleep.*
The moon king comes to take his queen.
Spirit to bone, ghost to flesh.
He claims his bride.
Never wake again."

I threw the mouse on my bed. Then, without a care in the world, I forwarded the email to my entire contacts list, too exhausted to type individual email addresses in. *Shit, was that my school email? Ugh. Whatever.* I grabbed a Listerine strip from my purse, letting it dissolve on my tongue as I settled into bed and turned out the light. I took a hit from my bowl, making my face glow orange and blowing the smoke out slowly. Then, I shoved the pillow firmly over my face.

"Ugh... *naked*... right. I'll meet you halfway."

I slid my hands from my pillow to my hips, tucking my thumbs under my panties. I tugged them down, keeping them around one ankle. I pulled my shirt up, exposing my breasts. My cheeks flushed for a moment, not feeling great about having my breasts out. They were nothing special, and I figured if the demon was real, he'd be disappointed after seeing Neveah's rack. I tugged the comforter to my chin.

"Can I please sleep now?" I begged in a hoarse voice, feeling stupid that I was talking to a spirit that probably didn't exist after all. But a few seconds later, a cold fingertip skated up my belly, and a hand cupped my breast. I froze at the unmistakable feeling of my nipple being tugged. I gasped. My eyes were wide, and I waited for anything to happen again. Anything that couldn't be explained by a draft or rough sheets.

"Open," a voice whispered excitedly into my neck. My breath hitched. "Obey me." I was too scared to move. Impatient with my lack of compliance, the cold hand gripped my inner thigh hard, and I yelped. He pushed my thigh open.

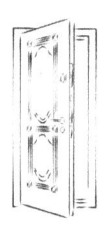

"No..." I pleaded, my voice cracking. I had made a grave mistake. Regret and dread were a dry knot in my throat. But the fingers caressed my center, finding my clit. I flinched. I tried to sit up and get away, but my muscles froze. I screamed briefly, and my voice quickly seized up. My jaw involuntarily clenched shut.

I was paralyzed, laying on my back with a leg pulled to the side. Large fingers spread my lips apart, massaging the gathering moisture up and over my clit. He grabbed my other thigh and squeezed it tight. He pushed that leg open even wider than the first. I sobbed quietly and panted as I fought to move, getting zero response. I was too tired to fight.

I was freezing. My nipples hardened painfully. Even the tear that fell from the corner of my eye felt like ice. He rubbed my clit, making me moan without thinking. That dinosaur-like growl rumbled between my legs, and terror consumed me. *What the hell is that?* I could see nothing in the dark room but a faint shadow between my legs. The invisible entity, the demon named Bane, played with my body like a cat with a dead mouse. I wondered how mangled I would be when he was done toying with me.

A long, wet appendage lapped at my lips, a breath away from my sensitive clit. I flinched again. He licked closer to the center of my pussy, and I squealed; the sensation conflicted with my terror. I tried to scream for him to stop, but it came out as a muffled screech as his tongue licked deep between my lips. I drew in a hot breath at the feeling of his wet tongue against me. My pussy heated, priming for him.

"That's it," he growled, devouring me.

I had never felt a tongue there, and my heart leaped. It pushed deep inside, extending the full depth and sliding in and out. As terrified as I was, there was no denying it felt incredible. With my fight or flight instincts electrifying all of my senses, I felt every lick with intensity. Conflicted, I thrashed as I squealed and begged with hoarse groans.

Then he licked a trail to my chest. As he took my nipple into his mouth, he pushed thick fingers inside of me. He hooked them forward, and the breath I released sounded like I was huffing in offense. But it was pure bliss and shock. I had never made that sound before. I had never been touched there before.

Another growl left his throat, a demonic purring that was sobering. *There is a fucking demon fingering me.* He nibbled on my nipple. My body trembled, and my breath hitched, hoping the pleasure I was experiencing wasn't angering him enough to hurt me. He slowly worked both fingers in and out of me in a maddening rhythm.

I yearned for the intense pleasure that hooking motion created. I could not let the memory of that feeling go as he proceeded to only give me simple thrusts. Shamefully, I became excited with anticipation. I wanted him to touch the spot again, the spot that made me want to curl my toes, even though I couldn't. He made a small motion to do it again, and my breath became deep and expectant.

He stopped. Instinctively, I tried to rock my hips to satisfy the need that was just out of reach. I couldn't. He was still, and I halted my breathing, afraid I had angered him. A hot tear fell, rolling down my cheek.

When he finally did move, I whimpered as he gently twisted his fingers in and out instead. The sound of my wetness was impossible to ignore, and my face turned hot. There was no hiding that he was arousing me. He licked my nipple again, finishing with a hard suck before tucking his face into my neck. My brows scrunched together at the tickle of the demon's mouth over my hammering pulse. My core tingled, and I caught a hardy breath in my throat. My face burned hot. He wanted to turn me on. He wanted to force me to cum for him. *Why? What would happen next?*

"Sleep for me," he ordered in a terrifying voice as he continued to rub his thumb over my clit gently. My eyelids grew heavy instantly, and my mind relaxed, amplifying the pleasure between my legs. I fought it, unsure if he would ever let me wake again. Was he seducing me to my death? I was sleep-deprived and weak. Fighting him was nearly impossible, but I gave it everything I had. He hooked his fingers again, and my eyes fell shut as I moaned and sobbed.

It was terrifying and amazing all at once. I didn't want this. Did I? Why was I getting so wet? Nothing good would come from submitting to a demon. My face burned with shame. I sunk into the plush mattress.

"Yes," he said, pushing his cold, thick fingers hard against that sensitive spot and rubbing it, his thumb massaging my clit faster. A squeal rushed past my lips. My breasts tightened, and my thighs ached to spread wider. "Sleep for me."

He fucked me with his fingers and stroked the underside of my swollen clit. My body bounced as his fingers reached the back of my pussy. He was lulling me into sleep with gentle, rocking thrusts. I realized that I had been moaning with each plunge, and my cheeks burned with embarrassment.

I had never cum before, but I knew that was what was building between my legs. I was eager to know how it felt but became nervous as my body responded to him with increasing ferocity. I didn't know what to expect. Every embarrassing thing that could go wrong raced through my mind as my pleasure barreled toward the unknown.

"No..." I breathed, not sure if I really meant it. His touch was a patient ecstasy. His laughing growl in my ear all but confirmed he would make me take it. I squirmed, trying to escape before my body betrayed me, and my climax gave way to whatever horrors he had in store.

"*Sleep* for me," he ordered again, and another wave of sleepiness weighed heavy on my mind. The approaching oblivion was euphoric, and my body tingled with calmness as he made me take his fingers harder. It was overwhelming. I wanted to throw my head back and grip the sheets, but I remained immobile. All I could do was moan louder. To my horror, my sounds of pleasure were husky and not at all feminine, but I couldn't stop. I was trapped, feeling the most overwhelming release I had ever experienced. My body, from pussy to thighs, surrendered to his touch. I was no longer fighting it but allowing myself to fall open for him.

I lost control. My inner walls clamped around his fingers as pleasure exploded in my core. Hot liquid coated his hands, and I hollered in shock. He hooked me again, pulling my body down the bed by the pelvic bone and lifting my hips high. He prodded that soft spot aggressively, making my wetness splash everywhere as he fingered me through my orgasm. It was the best thing I had ever felt. I screamed.

He growled and panted over my prone form, nothing more than a faint shadow. "My name..." he demanded.

"Bane!" I cried as carnal satisfaction undulated through my core. I screamed it again and moaned loudly for him. My voice cracked.

"Tell me you are mine."

I didn't care what the fuck that meant. I would say anything to make sure he didn't stop.

"Bane! I'm yours! I'm yours!" I mewled it over and over again as my orgasm ripped through me. As the sensations faded, my head became dizzy.

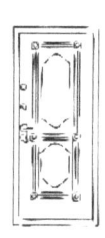

"*Sleep,*" he commanded more aggressively. Unable to fight him any longer, sleep consumed me. His fingers were still hooked inside my pussy, and he pulled me down hard into the mattress. He pulled me right through it until we fell through the midnight sky of the Dream World.

I lost all sense of direction; gravity seemed to pull at me from different angles, yet the wind was steady at my back. As my body slowly descended, my softening moans echoed endlessly. I landed gently on the diamond dust sand. I felt rested and alert, yet still unable to move save for a few parts of my face.

Oh no! The sand.

Bane was on top of me. I could see him. A massive, well-defined shoulder with silver-blue skin was just above my lips. His back was solid muscle, with a wide frame. He had sharp, silver horns protruding down his spine that became smaller the closer they got to his round ass. My knee lay limp by his hip, my legs spread wide at his waist. His arm was between us, sinking his fingers deeper.

I moaned softly as the remnants of my orgasm pulsed. Scared, I caught myself and tried to stay quiet. He did exactly as I had feared, driving me to desperation until he could trap me for God knows what reason.

He hissed in my ear. I tried to look at him. My body was still frozen, but I could move my head slightly. I needed to see him and get some sense of his soul. But his face was tucked against my neck, sucking and kissing. It felt nice. When he moved, his strong jawline tugged my bottom lip, and I wondered if it would be dangerous to move it away. I decided it was safer to be still and avoid provoking him.

If I gave him what he wanted, maybe I would survive. I studied him, unable to stop panting into his pointed ear and trying to be as quiet as possible as he massaged my soaked pussy. That's when I noticed his pointed ears were pierced with large gauges of beautiful crystal. He had black hair tied in a round bun, with the sides shaved. It seemed familiar. Had I seen him in a dream?

I had already cum, but he wasn't done touching me. It felt wrong to enjoy it. He wasn't trying to kill me yet, so I just waited as he petted me, adding more fingers occasionally and moaning into my neck as I winced from the stretch. It was nearly impossible to stay quiet as my body came alive again with his touch.

I tried to turn my head without him noticing so I could see more of him. He bit my earlobe hard, making me yelp; realizing I had angered him, my lips quivered. Warm blood trickled down my neck from the wound, and he licked it with his lengthy tongue. I could feel the forked tip, and my pussy flexed in excitement when I remembered how it felt inside me. I thought I heard him laugh, and he gently bit my neck. Internally, I cursed myself for letting him affect me and tried to calm myself with a breath. He plucked one of the purple flowers on the sand and tucked it behind my sore ear.

"Soon, my little dream, we will be together forever."

"Little... dream?" My mouth could move.

He pulled his fingers from me and grabbed his cock, guiding it to my center.

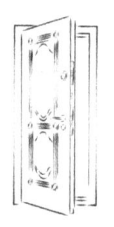

"Wait," I pleaded, a tear falling from my eye. My lips fanned around the head of the hard head of his cock. "Please. What's happening? What are you going to do to me? Please. Wait..."

"I have waited an eternity for you. Now open, and let me have my turn." He nudged his length between my legs. I cried out but caught myself and sucked in a few quick, shaky breaths to prepare. This was going to happen. I had no escape.

I closed my eyes and tried to clear my mind as he pushed. It couldn't even fit between my lips. It was wide enough to touch the sensitive skin between my thighs and pussy. But Bane kept pushing anyway, and my heart filled with dread, wondering if he would rip me open to fit.

A new terror came alive inside me. Something was prodding against my ass. It was hard and heavy, moving with serpentine motions as if it was impatiently waiting for its chance to dive into me. I let out a scared whimper, assuming a giant demon snake was ready to devour the scraps when Bane was done. It was like a pet ready to be let off its leash, lunging at my ass but just out of reach. My asshole tightened as the eager striking slapped against it. Bane seemed to ignore the wild thing.

He pushed forward again, harder this time, trying to thrust his beastly cock inside me, but my pussy couldn't accept him. He reached down with both hands, spreading my lips wide until they burned. He tried again. I winced. My slickness coated his tip, but he didn't fit. Bane growled loudly, breathing heavily with frustration as he thrust his hips eagerly over and over again, unable to get relief. My body trembled at the vicious sound and the soreness of my pussy stretching beyond its limits.

"Take me! Open for me now," the demon demanded; his lips were practically inside my ear as they pushed my cheek into the sand. He pulled me apart harder, and I yelped in pain. He thrust again, too hard. Our bodies were simply incompatible.

"I don't know how!" I cried.

He grabbed the top of my head for leverage and pushed me

down onto him. He was frenzied with need and growing angrier with my body's refusal.

"Do not lie to me! I *need* you; let me in."

As terrified as I was, I would be lying if I said my body didn't ache for him to fuck me. His rabid need was enticing. The way he kept telling me how badly he needed my pussy around his cock made me dizzy. The way he ripped flower-studded vines from the sand in frustration made my cheeks burn with passion. But it hurt. After what felt like an hour of the crazed demon trying to force my body to accept him, I couldn't take it anymore. Aching and sensitive, I begged him to stop.

"You're hurting me. Please... Please stop. You're going to tear me," I sobbed.

He let out a lion-like roar, punching the sand beside my head. I shrieked. He tucked his hips in hard, trying to force himself inside one last time. As he did, the snake-like thing lunged for my ass, making it just past the rim, and thrashed. My core melted instantly, and I drew in a deep breath. Fear struck my chest like lightning. I squirmed internally at the thought of a snake inside me. I screamed as it thrust forward again, and Bane hissed in excitement with each sound of terror.

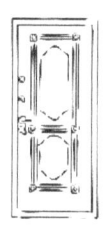

I woke to my alarm clock blaring. I shot up. My breaths were deep and anxious.

"It was a dream..." But I could feel cum puddling between my thighs. I looked under the sheets, seeing my panties still around my ankle and my top still pulled up. I touched myself; the tender flesh ached, and I hissed. My fingers slipped through the silver fluid on my center, and I lifted it to my tongue. My cheeks burned as I tasted what I somehow knew was Bane's metallic precum.

I pulled my shirt down and slipped my foot into the other leg hole of my underwear, pulling the fabric up. A flower fell from behind my ear. I flipped onto my hands and knees, turning around to find my pillow covered in broken vines studded in blooming purple flowers. More fell from my hair and onto my pillow. My face froze as I lifted my gaze to the flowers in the mason jar on my windowsill. *It was him. The flowers were from him. He's real. Everything was real.*

I was sore inside and out but not in immediate danger. The room was quiet, and I was well rested. My core was strangely relaxed and... relieved. My face was like stone as I stared at nothing. My mind was free of panic, and that concerned me the most.

I should be crying. Why am I not crying? What's wrong with me? How could I cum for him? Why aren't I crying? No one will believe me. I came... I didn't want to. I did want to, I think. I liked it. I screamed his name.

My eyes clenched shut momentarily as I remembered the noises I made for the demon. They were as loud in my memory as when I moaned them in his ear. I shook my head, remembering the feeling that drew them from me. Wetness leaked from my core as it flexed.

I sniffled and looked over at Neveah's bed, hoping she hadn't come home in case my wet dream was loud. Her bed was empty. I stood up, pressing my fingers against my sore pelvic bone to brace myself. I slowly exhaled as I turned around, worried that a sudden movement might cause terrible pain.

I plucked the flowers from the vines and set them in the makeshift vase. I couldn't say why I did it. I suppose I was simply going through the motions while waiting for the shock to wear off.

After discarding the vines in the trash, I made my bed, occasionally glancing at the Ouija board on the desk. *What the hell did Neveah let into our dorm room?*

I caught my reflection in my mirror and froze. I walked closer, grasping my ear lobe. It was torn and bleeding, and the hole was much bigger. I checked my other ear to find my earring hanging from a loose hole just the same.

6

BANE

I was ravenous. I had never needed a pussy wrapped around my cock so badly before. Buffy's terror was intoxicating. Her tears were like ecstasy on my tongue. But the way she cried and begged for me made my vision tunnel. I nearly blacked out from excitement, white specks floating from my periphery as I caught my breath and tried to give myself to her.

She was so fucking good. So when she disappeared from under me, leaving the head of my cock soaked and swollen, I screamed. She was gone, awake in her bed. The sun had risen in the human world, but I was ready to risk going blind to return to her. I punched the ground repeatedly, cursing and screaming. A plume of sparkling sand swirled around my large arm. I missed her. I needed her. My chest felt empty the moment she disappeared.

"Bane!" Slater called, running toward me as I continued my angry onslaught. "What is it?" Slater was a brother to me. We shared no blood, but he was my closest friend and confidant. Panting, I stared at the empty space below me before coming to a stand. My cocks were painfully hard, my bulb heavy.

"My dream. I had her! But she could not take me," I snarled, turning away and charging down the dark beach. What cruel joke had fate played on me?

Slater caught up, walking by my side. "It has been a long time since a sleep demon has paired with a human. You could not have known what to expect." He clapped his hand on my shoulder. "You look fit for war, brother. Some demonesses are still haunting; their bodies lie on the shore just a short walk away. See her there? She's a fine one. Fuck her until your human can take you."

I grumbled, stomping through the sand. I looked around, seeing the random bodies laid out. The beach was always scattered with them every quarter mile or so. It was always night here and always night *somewhere* in the human world. So, when a demon or demoness grew weak and needed to feed, or they wanted to produce seed to spawn with their partner, they came here to meditate until the power of the Sacred Sands took them to the human world to haunt.

"I do not want to fuck anyone but her. You can not understand until you have found your own dream. She is the only one who will satisfy me. I need her to adapt fast." I tugged at my cock, trying to hurt myself enough to get it to go down. It was no use. Her sweet whimpering seemed to echo in my ear. She was haunting *me*. I scoffed, walking faster.

"The master of healers will tell you how to do that, Bane. Stay patient. You do not want to kill her, do you?" He stepped over the limp body of the demoness he had pointed to before.

"Of course not. I would never hurt her if it was not necessary."

Slater laughed. "If I ever find my human, he will know pain as quickly as he will know the worst terror of his life. I will give him no mercy until he submits."

"I do not doubt that. The way you have described him, it sounds like he will give you a legendary fight."

Slater's cocks grew firm. He slowed his stride as we approached the body of a demon who was haunting, and I stopped short to see what he was after.

"I will catch up to you soon, brother," he said, rolling the demon on his stomach and kneeling between his legs. He took his larger cock in hand and guided it to the male's ass. With some spit, he forced it in and began thrusting impatiently. I stepped over the demon's jerking legs and shook my head. It took a long moment of walking to be out of earshot of Slater's grunting and the slapping of his hips against flesh.

Slater was a high-ranking demon, not just because of his association with me but because he was ruthless and skilled. If the demon he was taking were to wake up and fight it, he would know only regret. It was the order of things here, and nobody ever questioned it. We protected and provided for our people, and they submitted to those more powerful.

I was close to our main cavern, a palace of sorts. When I arrived at the dunes, the line of guards stepped to the side and kneeled on both knees. I passed them uninterested, determined to find the master healer. I approached the entrance, a large, black hole in the ground, and hurried in.

"Your grace," a deep voice called as I descended into the dark cavern. The blue flames of the torches provided enough illumination to see without harming our eyes. The yellow embers tossing off them sizzled against my skin. A silver face emerged in the light and greeted me, dipping his knee to touch the ground once and rising.

"Not now, Overton."

"It can not wait. We have only a few moons until Samhain. We need to delegate demons. The humans will be celebrating their Halloween and calling for us in droves. The doorways will be open to many."

"It is the same as it has been every year since the dawn of time. Is it not? What issue do you take now in this year, 1998?"

"We have too many on guard. The Sandman has not been heard from in months. What if he plans to attack?"

I laughed, charging forward through the long, torch-lit tunnel. "The Sandman and what army? All have forsaken him, and rightfully so. He is in exile because he cannot face the shame of his defeat," I stated plainly and turned on my heel. "Where is Khadijah?"

"She is leading lessons, of course."

"I need her. Call off lessons," I ordered as I reached the open main space. The window ceiling high above us let moonlight spill into the room. The ivory walls were wrapped tight in vines of beach morning glories in full bloom. Crystal accents adorned the floors and walls like buttons bolstering the ivory stone. The blue torches glowed on the indigo, velvet-lined furniture.

"The new healers need structure, Your Grace. How are they to heal anyone in their sleep without it? Certainly, this can w—"

I took Overton by the neck and slammed him into the wall, squashing the vines of blooming flowers that clung to it. "I have an immediate need to see our master healer," I said through clenched teeth. "Call off lessons and get Khadijah *now*."

"Of course, Your Grace," he answered with a smile. I released him, and he kneeled deep, touching his knee down for a long moment before leaving. He enjoyed making me snap, always a whore for terror.

He scurried away, and I contemplated offering him to Slater for a week. Perhaps he would stop playing games and learn some discipline so things could get done around here more efficiently. I crossed the space, high demons quickly touching a knee to the ground and rising slowly as I passed them.

I pushed open the doors to my study. The dark cavern walls were covered with luminous silver smoke that I had formed into images of Buffy. The images were from the dreams I had my entire adult life. I had been obsessed with her for a long while. My entire study was a shrine, lit only by her beauty. The smoke covered every inch of the walls and ceiling, Buffy's face swirling in different still frames from my memory.

On my desk lay the strand of hair I had pulled from her head, the panties I had stolen from her room, and the sand from the shore where I first tried to force myself into her. I grabbed the panties and wiped her cum off of my cock with them. Then I laid them out again, smoothing out the wrinkles.

I lit a new incense that was scented with orange blossoms and inhaled the smoke through my nose. I closed my eyes, remembering the confused and terrified look on Buffy's face as she came for me. I couldn't help but smile. When I blew the smoke out, it glowed and took the shape of that very image. I leaned back in my chair, stroking my cocks as I looked at her mouth, open wide, as I gave her what I was certain was her first orgasm.

The door swung open, and Khadijah came through. She glided

in front of me like a ghost and then slowly made to kneel as if she had real knees. Nobody knew what was under her loose, white robe, but it was clearly not a body like ours. She raised her chin. Her silver skin stretched over her eye sockets, yet I could feel her looking at me.

"My King. You have emergent business for me?" she asked, rising just as slowly.

I released my cocks and stood, moving Buffy's new image to a more private nook in the wall behind my desk. It lit up the space brightly. "I found my dream the other night. She is human, you know?" I began, turning from it reluctantly.

"I remember you mentioning that. What pleasant news. How may I help?"

"Her body will not accept me. It has been four nights since I found her. She is unchanged."

"It will take time, but she will begin to adapt as soon as she offers herself to you."

"She has offered herself to me. She has said she is mine. And still, she refused to open."

"She does not *refuse* you. She has no idea what is about to happen to her and is *incapable* of willing her body to do it. You must be patient. She must truly offer herself to you. Say it and agree to *bleed* for you. And tell her that it *will* hurt."

"How badly?"

"Excruciating. But there are some things you can do to move it along; still painful yet not as bad as allowing her to transform into a demoness on her own. Some things are better left to nature, I am afraid. Though silver supplements may help with that."

"How quickly can I change her into a demoness?"

"I will look through the scrolls to find what I can. In the meantime, I strongly suggest you haunt her from a distance. You are too wound up. If you try to force her again before her body is ready, you may kill her. She will bleed out before she is marked."

"That is what I tried to tell him," Slater interjected, walking in with his cocks gone limp, the spirited one groggy but snaking up his leg curiously. "But he would only listen to the great and wise *Khadijah*." He leaned toward the eyeless healer with a flirtatious grin. The male had always wondered what was under a healer's long robe that he could stick one of his cocks into. If she had eyes, she would have rolled them, but instead, she turned her chin away and pursed her lips.

"Slater will go with you. He's the finest mage we have. If there is a spell to move this along, he will sniff it out," I announced.

"Very well..." Khadijah murmured regretfully, gliding out of the room. Slater watched her leave and then turned back to me.

"How was your fuck?"

"He woke," he said, laughing to hide his disappointment. "I told him to hold still and let me finish, and he came on the spot, of course. Who does not love waking up to being fucked? No terror, but I filled him up quickly anyway."

"Glad to hear it." I rubbed the damp fabric of Buffy's panties between my finger and thumb.

"You know the Sandman went silent. There are whispers that—"

"Ugh. You, too, with the Sandman. The Sandman is a powerless coward who hides in some hovel. He may not be able to die, but he will live knowing he is useless."

"He *can* still be summoned by humans, brother. We need to bind him to this world before Samhain approaches. The humans celebrate Halloween earlier every year. Ouijas have never been more popular, and they scarcely understand their consequences. If he enters their world again… if he finds a human weak enough…it could be catastrophic."

I looked up at him for a moment and bit my lip. He was right. I was consumed by my gorgeous human, my perfect little dream, and was not thinking clearly. I sighed and leaned back in my chair, looking up at her many images splayed across the ceiling in smoke. I fixated on one of her beaming. It was like she was smiling down at *me* right now. I would make her smile like that every day, soon enough. "Send a few squads out to search the old caverns and the highlands."

"And how many are we reserving for Samhain?"

"Pull from the detail for the cavern of Sacred Sands. A hundred guards for one cavern has always been overkill."

"May I make a suggestion?"

"You will anyway."

"Keep the Sacred Sands guarded by a hundred. Send the filches to scout for the Sandman. They are powerless sleepers but immortal. We will not waste resources for the summonings or compromise the sands."

"This is why *you* are my force advisor. Let Overton know and get to Kahdijah quickly," I said. "And Slater. Stop taunting her. The healers are off limits."

He sucked his fangs playfully and touched a knee to the ground before leaving.

As soon as the door closed, I turned back to my newest image of Buffy. I sat in my chair, grabbed a cock in each hand, and stroked myself to the memory of her fighting her climax. She was perfect. Her terror was immaculate.

If anyone ever touched her, I would carve them into cubes and feed them to the filches. She was mine, and I had every intention of tormenting her until my perfect little dream broke. By the time I was through torturing her, she would be begging to bleed for me, offering herself desperately. I smiled, counting down the minutes until the sun set on her side of the human world.

7

BUFFY

It had been four days since I was last haunted, and again, I hadn't been able to sleep. Aside from the flowers Bane left on my pillow while I was away, he hadn't visited me again. Every day, the sleep deprivation got more unbearable, chipping away at my mind. Since I last saw him, I refused to be naked and avoided the shower, too. I felt disgusting. Every time I went to open my emails, I had a sense of impending doom until I confirmed there were none from "unknown sender." For some reason, it caused a pang of disappointment, too.

The first night without sleep wasn't terrible. I was drowsy, and my eyes felt itchy, but I stayed awake on purpose and avoided my dorm, crashing at Harvey's place. Even there, I felt like I was being watched. The air smelled metallic, and I couldn't get warm, no matter how many blankets and jackets I covered myself with. I brushed it off.

But what I couldn't ignore was the constant replaying of what he did to me the night before and how good it felt. I lay awake, hugging a pillow and trying to understand how I could have enjoyed it. *It's just a reflex. It doesn't mean I let him make me cum. It is an uncontrollable reflex.*

I could only hide in Harvey's dorm for so long before rumors would start to circulate that I was a slut, or his roommate would complain about the regular company. I didn't need any of that. So, I decided to face my fears and go back to my own dorm.

That second night was rough. My body was exhausted, but my mind wouldn't turn off. When I closed my eyes, my lids would twitch and jerk. Against the blackness, all I could see were images of what he did to me. My center heated, and I thought I heard the demon laughing. Then I thought I felt a brush against my ankle. I jumped in panic and lay awake with my back against the wall. Every sound I heard that night made my stomach lurch and, somehow, made me excited that he maybe hadn't gotten bored of me.

The next day, I started feeling very off. I was late for class, dragging my feet and forgetting the right books. I was clumsy and forgetful. I thought about Bane constantly, and shame consumed me as my center ached for the release he had given me.

That third night without sleep was worse. I hadn't showered, and I smelled like Harvey's gym bag after a game. My skin was crawling, and my oily scalp itched. As exhausted as I was, I couldn't manage to sleep. I twirled the newest flower in my fingers and swallowed hard. He was doing this to me. He was keeping me awake so I would bend to his will. He was wearing me down, debasing me, and taunting me. What did he want?

The following day was when I truly started to spiral. Skeeter caught me losing my balance on the way back to my dorm and offered to help me, scooping his arm under mine. I leaned on him, the fatigue distracting me from his disingenuous comfort. By the time he helped me stumble to my door with my bloodshot eyes barely open, he had his hands halfway up my shirt, and he smirked. I shook my head, removed his hand, and turned to unlock my door. My vision doubled, and I struggled to guide the key into the lock.

"Don't be like that, Buffy. Let me help you relax. I can put you to sleep. Promise," he said, snaking his arms around me and slipping his hand down the front of my baggy pants.

I cringed. "Stop it. I need to go to bed." I felt for the slit in the knob with my thumb and guided the key against it. Finally, it slipped into the hole, but it seemed to be stuck. Was it upside down? I couldn't see well enough to tell.

Skeeter laughed, ignoring how I tried to squirm out of his hold as I tugged on the key impatiently. He made my skin crawl. When Bane forced me to receive his touch, I didn't feel this disgusted, angry, or *annoyed*. I wondered if I really disliked Bane at all or if I was just terrified of the unknown. I shook off the dangerous thought.

"Let's lay down together, huh? I'll be quick. You'll sleep so good, watch."

"No," I said flatly, tugging on his wrist, but he resisted. He pushed it further down, rubbing my left labia over my panties. *Why is it always the left lip?*

"No? You don't like when I play with your pussy like this?" He laughed into my neck.

Gag. I snapped, turning around and shoving him hard. "Get off of me! I'm not interested. Got it? Jesus, Skeeter. Take a fucking hint and keep your hands off of me! I shouldn't have to tell you three fucking times. I said no! Why the hell do you think it's okay to stick your hands down my pants? Huh? You think you own me or something? You *suck* in bed! Okay? I didn't even want to the first time. It's not happening again!"

I never yelled. I never punched that low. I never went off on long, unhinged rants because of a simple problem I could absolutely handle more calmly. But the lack of sleep had made me light on the trigger. I didn't care if I hurt his feelings either. He deserved it. Maybe he'd think twice before trying to wear down the next girl. He was crossing the line into assault at this point. And just like that, I caught myself craving Bane's force again. *I need so much therapy.*

Skeeter stood with his hands up in surrender, his face hollow with shock. I thought I saw the shadow of a large demon down the hall, and chills ran up my spine. I heard a growl, and the atmosphere became cold and charged. It was sobering, but for some reason, my heart fluttered.

"Fuck, man. You on the rag or something?"

"Get out of here, Skeeter," I warned calmly, my glossy red eyes darting up and down the hall for any sign of Bane. It was not lost on me that I would rather be alone with the demon than this creep. "You should stay away from me... Or you might get hurt."

"You know what, Buffy, I'm a good guy. Your loss, you crazy bitch," he said, backing away and turning. "You can fuck Harvey and the whole football team, but not me. Got it!" he yelled loud enough for anyone to hear as he stormed down the hall. I knew sleeping at Harvey's was a bad idea. "*Slut!*"

I shut the door behind me and fell into my bed, crying. I was desperate for sleep and unable to work through the emotions of that pathetic creep trying to take advantage of me. Coldness pressed against my back. Like a cold washcloth over my head, it calmed me. And then it was gone; the flowers on my pillow were still ice cold. I stared at them, the last thread of my sanity growing more precarious with every blink.

That was how the fourth night started. I lay awake with my eyes wide open. I tried to remember the shape of the shadow that caught my eye in the hall. Why had the fear of his presence excited me? Why was I fighting the urge to touch myself the way he did? Could I touch myself the way he did? Would I finally sleep if I did? Thinking of his predatory growl, I lowered my hand but stopped. What if he was watching? What if I was imagining his shadow, and he had forgotten about me days ago? A pit grew in my stomach.

The following morning, I could tell I was very unwell. My mind was coming undone, and my thoughts were slow and repetitive. My vision was tilting, blurring, and doubling. The memories from that night were fragments, so vivid and unsolicited that I thought they were happening all over again.

I was also, for whatever reason, embarrassed. It's not like I consented to it, so why should I care if he couldn't satisfy himself inside me? If he couldn't take his "turn," as he said. Why should I be concerned that he thought I wasn't desirable after my body couldn't accommodate him? I worried about how angry he was when it ended. If he ever got ahold of me again, he would definitely cut me open just to fit or let the snake inside me. The thought made my thighs clench in fear, and I shivered. So, why the hell was I so obsessed? I kept my shameful fantasies tucked safely away in my mind, never to act on them.

I couldn't pay attention in my lecture. The memory of Bane was louder than Mr. Feeny, who was only a few feet in front of me. I rubbed my tired eyes and fought the hundredth yawn of the day, chugging the rest of my Surge soft drink. My body slumped as I checked my Giga Pet. It was dead. I killed it. I was too tired to care. *Better it than me... Would he kill me?* The most he had hurt me was by biting. He could have torn me if he wanted to, but he took the time to stretch me.

"Any questions?" Mr. Feeny asked with a minute left until the class ended. I woke from my daydream, cursing myself for not paying attention.

"Ms. Fatone, a word?" he said as I slung my bag on my shoulder. I turned on my heel, swaying a bit and squinting. The light had been hurting my eyes worse with each passing day.

"Yes?" I said, faking a smile.

"You're a bit distracted lately. You look unwell. You're not engaging in discussions. Your homework is late. What is going on?"

"Homework?" I slapped my hand on my forehead. "The diagram of the heart! I'm so sorry. Can I have an extension? I'll get it done by the next class."

"I can't give you an extension. I would have to give everyone one. Whatever is going on with you, snap out of it, kiddo. Finals are just around the corner, and you're on track to graduate with honors."

"Yeah." I nodded and turned to the door. I didn't even care that I was graduating with honors. Then again, I never cared about college. Despite how easy school was for me and how happy I was to have the option to be one of those independent women, I just wanted to be a stay-at-home mom with a bunch of kids. But men *sucked*, and feminists would probably judge me for it, so I tried to let the promise of honors motivate me.

It was late. I was barely able to speak clearly or walk straight. But the thought of going to my haunted dorm when I was this weak scared me. I had no self-defense anymore. So, even though I had a really cool new computer, I headed to the library to use one of theirs instead.

I stopped at the campus store for a snack, yet I couldn't remember how I got there. I plopped mineral water, Benadryl, melatonin, Unisom, and a blueberry muffin on the counter. *Oh yeah.* I was determined to sleep tonight, even if it landed me in the hospital. The cashier knotted her brow and looked at me in concern as she rang them up. As the scanner beeped, my mind drifted.

I glanced at a rack of earrings on display. My eyes caught a set of clear gauges. Memories of Bane's pointy ear with large, round crystal gauges flashed through my mind, and I heard myself moaning loudly into his ear. I startled. The cashier looked at me sideways. Did she hear it, too? Was it in my mind, or did I moan out loud just then? I couldn't even tell.

"Ma'am?"

My eyes were tunneling as I started to panic. I could hear nothing but our carnal ecstasy. It was too loud. Someone would hear.

"Ma'am?"

His growling filled my ear, and my breath quickened. *Is he here? Am I moaning out loud? Am I yelling his name? Am I lying down or standing?*

"Ma'am? Is that all?" The cashier's words broke me from my stupor.

I looked at her slack-jawed and panting. "Huh? Is that... all... um." I grabbed the 8mm gauges from the rack. "These, too, please," I mumbled.

I had never stretched my ears, but the holes seemed wider since that morning. As I walked away from the store, I pushed my new gauges in easily. Checking them in my compact mirror, I smiled, wondering if Bane would like them. Then, I caught the dark circles carved out under my eyes. *God, I need sleep. I'm going fucking crazy.*

I don't remember walking to the library either, but I made it there. I sat at the public computer and logged into my school email. The words seemed to scramble before my eyes. There was a reminder to bring my ID to the testing center and a number two pencil for the scantron. *What test do I have? What's today?* Then, there was an email from Mr. Feeny, who offered extra credit to the class, which was due promptly after the Halloween Break.

"*Yes,*" I whispered, hoping I wasn't imagining it. I starred the email to read again later, after I, hopefully, slept.

Then, I opened my personal email. I froze, rubbing my heavy eyes in disbelief. My face tingled with fear. My blood ran cold as I opened the message from an unknown sender.

It read:

> SLEEP NAKED TONIGHT. LEAVE YOUR WINDOW OPEN AND YOUR WATER ON THE WINDOWSILL. SEND THIS POEM TO THREE FRIENDS, OR YOU WILL NEVER SLEEP AGAIN.
> READ IT OUT LOUD:
> RISE, RISE, DEMON OF SLEEP.
> TAKE HER BODY, YOURS TO KEEP.
> CRACK THE BONE AND RIP THE FLESH
> BECOME HIS BRIDE,
> NEVER WAKE AGAIN"

I read the email under my breath and repeated the third verse in horror. "Crack the bone..." I recoiled. "Rip the flesh?" My mouth soured. There was no way I could let him near me.

But what if this was a prank? Someone could have been getting back at me for the first one I sent. I did basically send it to the entire campus. Or maybe it was Skeeter, pissed that I wouldn't put out yesterday. I wasn't computer savvy, but I knew a few people who were. I forwarded the email to Harvey first.

> 'HEY, IS THERE ANY WAY TO TRACK WHO IS SENDING ME THESE EMAILS?'

I wrote.

I gnawed on my lip, impatient. Thoughtlessly, I forwarded it to a few other computer-savvy friends, too.

Yawning, I logged off and moved the keyboard so I could read a few chapters from my microbiology book. I reread the same sentences over and over without actually reading them. I absorbed *none* of it. The pictures seemed to move. My eyelids were heavy, and I closed them, nodding off for a few seconds. But then I heard his laugh and was startled awake. *No...*

I was so close to sleep. I couldn't last like this. And I couldn't avoid the shower forever, either. I gathered my belongings, determined to get back, shower and rest without being haunted.

"Excuse me," the librarian said as I turned to walk away. "If you can't respect our equipment, then don't use it. This will be your only warning."

I looked at the keyboard that she motioned to. Some of the keys were pulled off and sitting on the desk, lined up like scrabble letters. I shook my head.

"I don't know how that happened. I'm so sorry," I mumbled, sounding like a drunk person. I walked over to replace them. There were three keys arranged to say '2 AM.' When I grabbed them, they were like ice. I shuddered, pressing them back into place as the librarian shook her head with her arms crossed. She walked away, muttering something to herself. When I turned back around, a morning glory rested on the table where my book was. My brain knew this was not a good thing. The excitement I felt could only be explained by severe sleep deprivation. *I'm in danger. I should run now.*

I grabbed my things and rushed out into the night, leaving the flower behind. The campus looked deserted. I glanced at my watch. It had died, stuck at 2:00 am, for the third night in a row. *It's a coincidence. You just need sleep, Buffy.*

Shadows swallowed me as I walked between buildings, and something moved out of the corner of my eye. I spun in the alleyway, stumbling against the brick building. No one was there. When I hurried to cross a large parking lot, the wind rustled the leaves on the trees, and I shivered. My footsteps seemed louder for some reason. I could feel eyes on me. I stayed on high alert, staring forward and picking up my pace.

It became too much; I had to look back. A large man with the same bulky frame as Bane stood shrouded in darkness under a tree. I gasped and stumbled. He cocked his head and stepped forward. A pale blue shoulder appeared in the moonlight.

I ran. I ran as fast as I could through the lot and between two buildings. I could hear his laugh behind me before he groaned ever closer. I squealed, my tears destroying my heavy black eyeliner. I turned the corner quickly and panted as I ran for my life. Someone grabbed my arm, pulling me to a screeching halt. I nearly fell, screaming and jumping in fear. The grip held firm, and I spun.

"Relax, Buffy. It's just me!" Harvey said. His kind blue eyes looked me over. "Are you okay? What are you running from?"

"Someone's following me," I explained through my sobs. My knees gave out as I bunched his letterman jacket tightly in my fist, but he caught me. I wiped a tear from my cheek and cried harder. He looked around, his arms pressing me against him tightly.

"Where are they? I'll handle them, Buff. I got you."

I looked to either side, sniffling and trembling. No one was there. Or at least my eyes wouldn't focus long enough to see if there was. I caught my breath and swallowed dryly, turning back to him.

"I... I don't know. I saw someone hanging out under a tree and... It's nothing," I stammered, rubbing my tired eyes. My voice cracked. "I haven't slept in days, Harv. I think I'm going crazy. I'm just really paranoid right now."

"I would be, too, if I was getting those emails. There's no IP address, not even for wherever you forwarded it from."

"So, how do I find out who is sending them?"

"I'm not sure, Buff, but it's 1:00 am. We won't find the answers tonight. I can try looking into it in the morning. Why don't I walk you to your dorm, huh? You need to get some rest."

I nodded, ducking under his arm and slowly walking with him. I didn't miss the way he turned his nose to my body odor, though he was nice enough not to say anything. He was warm. Usually, I hated the heat, but Harvey's warmth was easy and comforting. I glanced over my shoulder, looking for any sign of Bane. There was nothing.

We ambled back slowly, my balance worse than a freshman who snuck into a bar. He held me against him, talking about his football team's drama. Spencer caught the clap and put all four of his one-night stands in a group chat to tell them. Justin may have knocked up a sorority girl and didn't know if he should tell his girlfriend back home. Before I knew it, I had forgotten what happened and was even laughing.

"And you know that guy Skeeter you used to see? You know he's missing?"

"What? What do you mean?"

"I mean, they found his car in the parking garage with a bunch of blood on the driver's seat, and nobody has seen him since last night."

I shook my head. "That's... really scary. I hope he's okay."

No, I didn't. I couldn't care less. He probably got handsy with the wrong girl. *I'm a terrible person.* Finally, we reached my dorm.

"Hey, do you have any pot?" I asked as we got to my door. Harvey fished through his pocket, pulling out a joint.

"Crippy on me," he said, smiling. I took it from him with a thankful yet tired grin.

"Do you want to come in and smoke?" I asked, not wanting to be alone.

"No. Thanks though. I have an exam in the morning. Smoke me out next week?"

"Yeah, cool beans. Thanks again, Harv." I hugged him and gave him a kiss on the cheek.

"Hey, nice earrings, by the way," he said as he walked away.

"Thanks." I blushed as I rubbed the gauges and remembered Bane on top of me.

I walked through the door, and to my absolute dismay, Neveah and Skyler were fucking around with the Ouija board again. They looked up at me, instantly noticing the disapproval on my face.

"I was just about to leave," Skyler said, looking at the ground and leaving unceremoniously. Neveah looked down-right pissed, her casted arm hanging out of an ugly, dark blue sling.

"What was that about?" I asked, walking in slowly and dumping my bag on the bed.

"The chain letters you're sending are super fucked, you know that?"

"I haven't sent you one recently."

"The new one about *'breaking bones?'* It's made rounds." She tucked the Ouija board in its box. I ignored her comment but eyed the board nervously.

"Didn't have fun summoning demons today?" I asked, ripping open the grocery bag and fishing out the sleep aids.

"Did you break my arm?"

I spun around, mouth gaping. "No! I absolutely did not!"

"Oh, yeah?" She threw her notebook at me with her good arm. It hit my shoulder and fell to the ground. The pages fluttered open, revealing words scribbled all over them.

"I asked him how I broke my arm!"

Picking the notebook up, I stared at it.

> Don't touch her again.
> Stay out of her things.
> Stay quiet.

"You were the only one in here that night. I locked the door when I came home. And as you said, my arm was fine.

"I didn't touch you." I tossed her notebook back on the floor. My head throbbed. "And since when do you believe in the board?" I plopped on my bed, exhaustion taking over. I pulled out the joint that Harvey gave me and lit it up, sucking in a long hit. Coughing hard, I felt it almost instantly and smothered the tip in an ashtray.

"Something is going on, Buffy. It knows things no one else does. It outed Brandy for having feelings for me. She left, freaked out! And your little demon friend just informed me that Skyler has been fucking Tommy!"

"Why does that not surprise me in the least?" I muttered.

"It's not funny! It's fucking obsessed with you, and it moves on its own—"

Neveah yawned loudly. One moment, she was livid and yelling about Bane being real. The next, she was swaying and struggling to keep her eyes open. She groaned and turned to lie down. I furrowed my brows and tilted my head, realizing she was asleep already.

"Good talk…" I muttered sarcastically. *That was weird.* I bit my lip, picked up her notebook again, and flipped through the last few pages to see what else Bane had said to her.

Where is she?
I need her.
My little dream.
Buffy.
I need her.
She's mine.
Get her.
I need her.
Where is she?
Buffy.
Buffy.
Buf–

Why did my heart flutter? It seemed Bane hadn't stopped

thinking of me just as much as I hadn't stopped thinking of him. He was clearly dangerous and obsessed. But it almost sounded like he cared. Would he really hurt me? *If I could talk to him.*

I set my water down on the desk, the condensation soaking into the wood. I couldn't go on like this. I needed a shower and sleep. I'd sort out the rest in the morning. I turned to go to the bathroom but paused, turning back with the new chain mail in mind.

I wasn't sure if I wanted to have those dreams again or chance being killed. But I knew he wouldn't let me sleep if I ignored him. My only choices were to either try to talk to him or fight it and possibly die of exhaustion.

I reluctantly pulled back the makeshift fabric curtain, propping it open on my computer monitor. Then, I placed the water bottle on the ledge next to the mason jar of flowers. I unlatched the locks, lifting the window. It squeaked and skidded open. A cold breeze brushed across my skin, and the moonlight glistened over the water. I stumbled back, stupidly hoping it made him happy enough to be gentle and patient. I was also stupidly thinking this meant I wouldn't end up as a living sacrifice.

Grabbing my towel and toiletries, I headed for the shower. The community bathroom was empty. I hadn't been able to get warm for days, and I sighed as the water heated my skin, turning it pink. I took my time washing and conditioning my hair, scrubbing my nails into my scalp, and combing my fingers through the tangled knots. And, just in case, I shaved my legs and lips. It didn't mean anything. The soap rolled down my skin as I rinsed under the steaming water. It was my first shower in days, and I thoroughly enjoyed it.

The room had become thick with steam, and I could hardly see the other side of the washroom. Even though I was done, I wanted to stay under the water for a little longer. Suddenly, the lights flickered and went out. I spun, walking out from under the water. I widened my tired eyes in the darkness, trying to see anything, but they just burned with exhaustion. A clanging came from one side of the bathroom and again somewhere else. I trembled but was too tired to stiffen.

Hugging myself weakly, I cowered. "Hello?" I said nervously. No one answered. I turned the water off. My voice was weak. *"Hello?"*

I squeezed my hair out, ready to grab my towel. But a cold hand grabbed my side, just under my breast. I gasped, sucking in the steam. He nudged me slowly against the cold wall. *Oh fuck, he's touching me. And... I think I like it.*

"It's time to sleep, my little dream." His demonic voice echoed off the tile. *Sleep?* My breath hitched with excitement, water dripping off of my lips. Hot tears ran down my cheek at the thought of sweet, *sweet* sleep. His touch was gentle. He wasn't here to hurt me. *Was he?*

"Bane?" I whispered, reaching forward. I felt him, not just as staticky cold but his solid body. Leaning into him, I rested my wet face against his cool chest. I was desperate for him to let me sleep right then and there. My knees could have given out at any moment. My eyes fell shut like a magnet sticking to a fridge.

"Please don't hurt me," I whispered. I took a few deep breaths as he pulled me closer to him. My wet, naked body pressed against his with every inhale. I shivered from head to toe and spoke through chattering teeth. "I'll do whatever you want. Please. Please just let me sleep."

"You will crawl to me." He disappeared with a haunting laugh, scratching my skin as he dissipated. I pressed my fingers into the mark to dull the pain and found myself wanting to feel his arms around me again. I felt myself painfully awake and alone. Dread filled me. *I scared him away...* My eyes burned as tears fell faster.

"No... please. I'll do anything! I need to sleep. Please," I begged in the dark bathroom.

Patting the wall, I found my towel quickly and pulled it around my body. The thin terrycloth barely absorbed the water on my skin. As soon as I found the door, I stumbled out of the bathroom and toward my room. The hall was dark, glowing red from emergency exit signs. The electricity was out everywhere.

As soon as I entered, I was met with a wall of cold air. The dorm was dimly lit from the window, and Neveah was zonked. I locked the door and slowly padded forward, feeling his eyes on me. My stomach was in knots as I walked toward my bed, sniffling. I had laid out a 3xL Sublime t-shirt and some lacy black boyshorts. Instead, I let my towel fall loose, draping it over my computer chair. I had no choice. I could not function another day without rest and had to give in.

8

BUFFY

With chattering teeth, I pulled the Ouija board from under Neveah's bed, my wet hair dripping onto its surface. On my knees, I held the mouse between my breasts and turned. *You will crawl to me.* Is that what he wanted? Desperate, I clutched the mouse and crawled on all fours across the room. The air charged tremendously with every inch I gained. *He likes this. I can feel it.* I looked up, searching for him as I crawled to my bed. I could see no one, but felt his eyes on my shivering, naked body. My center heated and shame prickled at my cheeks.

The air was unbearably freezing by the time I reached the bed and crawled into it. Ice stiffened my wet hair. The moonlight pouring through the window made the crystal window on the mouse shimmer. I could smell the crisp autumn air from outside and hear the dead leaves rustling in the wind.

I lay flat, pulling the covers over me and shivering nervously, my breath clouding in the air. *So, this is how I die?* There was no questioning it; I was offering my body to a demon.

"Please... Bane. I'll do anything. Come back," I cried as hot tears rolled into my ears. My cheeks flushed when nothing happened. I hugged myself and felt entirely ridiculous.

But then I felt the air charged again, and my nostrils dried. I grew nervous and waited for him to realize he had broken me. I waited for him to touch me, hoping it wouldn't hurt. The knot in my throat made it hard to swallow. Then I felt a tug on my earlobe, the new gauges snug between his fingers. I flinched, but relief washed over me. *He's here. I can still convince him to let me sleep.*

"You offer yourself to me?" he asked, kissing my jaw. My face heated. I nodded without thinking. "It will hurt."

"What do you want from me?" I whispered with a shaky breath.

"To mark you."

"Why? What for?"

"We will talk more at home." He tugged my hair, tilting my head back. "*Sleep,*" he whispered.

I couldn't comply fast enough. I didn't fight him this time. Sleep consumed me. Instantly, I felt relief, rest, and comfort. I was falling slowly toward the sand and relaxing in his arms as he leaned in to kiss me. His tongue slid into my mouth, his fingers woven into my damp hair. The world around us was miles away, as I was lost in the hypnosis of his lips on mine. Every sick fantasy I had about him came rushing to the forefront of my mind as my heart hammered against my ribs. *Why is he kissing me so sweetly?* If I was being honest with myself, I loved it. I kissed him back nervously, and even though I could feel my hair tossing in the wind as we fell, we were all that seemed to exist at that moment.

Finally, we landed, the diamond-dust sand kicking up in the air and sparkling. It seemed to never fall, just glistening around us in the moonlight. His lips lifted off of mine. The moon was to his back, but I could make out his face. He was breathtaking and terrifying all at once. His sclerae were black, irises ocean blue with black slits for pupils. He had two large, silver spike piercings on either side of his pouty bottom lip.

He traced a palm over my breast. "You will be mine. The Demoness of Sleep. Let me into you."

"I don't know what any of this means, and I'm scared," I admitted, hoping that honesty and compliance would get me somewhere other than mauled.

He smiled, pulling up one side of his mouth as he glanced at my lips. "I know."

My stomach did somersaults looking at his gorgeous smirk. Two sharp fangs sprung out from his perfectly straight smile. I *have* dreamt of him before. I knew I must have. He seemed so familiar. He lowered himself down my body, leaving a trail of kisses as he went. Somehow, telling him I was scared had excited him.

His tongue trailed up my leg, and he let out a haunting growl. He wanted me. I could make him happy and keep sleeping. That wasn't a terrible trade, *right?* It's not like I had a virtue to protect. And he was honestly the most beautiful thing I had ever seen. My core heated.

Shamefully eager, I spread my legs slightly, and he pressed them open wider. Suddenly, I couldn't move my body, and fear crept over me again.

A haunting laugh rumbled from between my thighs as his tongue moved along my lips but did not part them. I drew in a deep breath, bracing myself. He tasted how wet I was and growled.

"What are you going to do to me?" I asked, trying to keep my breath steady. He laughed again. "Please, talk to me. I'm scared, and I need to know what you're going to do... after." He licked again, and my next breath came out harshly. I was wide awake and terrified, yet I didn't want it to stop. I was addicted to his terror.

"Open for me," he ordered before licking up my center, his tongue finally going between my lips.

I moaned. It felt amazing, chilled and wet. "What do you wan —?"

He did it again, pressing my legs open wider. He sucked my clit. I tried to arch my back, but I couldn't move. He would do as he pleased and make me agonize internally.

"Oh fuck," I groaned. He hummed in enjoyment. "Please... I jus —" He licked again, and I let out a breathy moan. "I'm scared..."

His fingers dug into my hips with eagerness, and he sucked my clit harder.

"Open for me," he demanded. His thick, forked tongue worked

over my clit. I groaned as the long length of his tongue slid deep inside. His face was buried in my wet heat as he tongue-fucked my pussy. He sucked my clit into his mouth again, pulling it between his lips until it popped free. I moaned louder. It was incredible.

"I am going to fuck you now. Do you like that?"

I panted, staying silent. I didn't know what I wanted until he licked me again. "Yes! Fuck." I felt pathetic. All he had to do was work me over with his tongue, and I was behaving like a desperate slut.

"Will you open for me?" He licked again.

"Ah! Yes. I will. I'll try. I... I promise."

Then, a sharp pain ripped through my center. I winced and cried out. It only lasted a moment.

"That's it. Open for me," he encouraged. "Open."

"O... Okay," I said mindlessly. Another sharp pain ripped across my hips, making a cracking noise. I screamed, but the ache dulled quickly.

"You are doing so well. Work through it."

He licked me every ten seconds, not enough to make me cum, but enough to drive me mad with need. I was making noises I had never heard myself make before. Every so often, the stabbing pain and crunching bone would jolt me. He paused and kissed my thighs.

"It will pass; just breathe." Then he licked me again and again, diving his long tongue inside periodically until I forgot about the pain.

Then he stopped. I tried to make my legs open wider, eager for more, but I was still immobile. Bane climbed on top of me, tasting every inch of skin on the way. He was unlike any lover I had before, and I knew with certainty that he could please me. I relaxed, but my body trembled with excitement.

"Spread your lips for me, my little dream."

"I... can't move when I'm with you," I said, staring up in awe at his beautiful face.

"You can move when I *let* you. When I tell you to. *S*pread your lips for me." He combed his fingers through my hair, and I couldn't stop staring at him. He grew impatient and growled. My breath hitched. With much effort, I reached between my legs with both hands and pulled my lips apart. My fingers slipped in the wetness, and I struggled to find enough friction to spread them. Heat was radiating off of my center.

"You won't fit." My mouth quivered. "I can't change that. I'm sorry."

He nudged his massive cock at my entrance, and I braced myself as he reached under me, leveraging my shoulders to push as hard as he could. He didn't fit. My heart raced, wondering what he might do.

"Let me in," he warned, brushing his lips against my ear. I loved the way they felt, and my eyes rolled back. His voice was like ecstasy. I wanted to let him in. I relaxed my center and spread my slick lips wider.

"I'm trying," I replied.

"I *need* you," he growled impatiently. My eyes rolled back again, and my cheeks flushed. I needed him, too. So fucking bad. He tried again to push into me, groaning, but could make it no farther. He punched at the sand and pulled back, sitting up. I yelped but kept my lips spread to show him my efforts. That's when I saw it. His cock was nearly the size of a two-liter. A large round bulb, the size of a mandarin orange, sat on the top, a quarter way up from the base.

Under his massive cock, where a human man's balls would be, was a second one. It was smaller than the first but still as long and thick as my forearm. It was squirming and seemed to have a mind of its own. The longer I looked at it, actually, the more certain I was that it *did* have a mind of its own. I realized that must have been what was writhing against my ass last time. Not a snake, but a sentient cock that seemed to have an affinity for assholes.

My jaw hung open as my tight hole clenched. The moisture from my center dripped down, soaking it. The sentient cock noticed and lunged for it eagerly, striking like a snake. I yelped and managed to buck out of the way. Bane seemed to be amused by my struggle, smirking at my fleching body and whimpers. He grabbed the sentient cock and squeezed it hard until it calmed, but I still trembled.

He looked down at me and grabbed my legs, shoving them upward, and inched his second cock toward my ass.

"Fine. I will have your ass tonight. But your cunt will take me soon, my little dream," he said. My eyes went wide. *My ass?*

"I can't! I haven't done... I can't just..."

Bane spit on his second cock and massaged it over the head. It thrashed in his hand excitedly, and he smiled at it.

"Calm down," he said to it. Then he gripped it tight to tame it again. It quivered as he nudged it against my tight hole.

"Wait! *No. No. No.* I can't." I willed my body to flinch, but I was trapped. My legs were paralyzed and resting on his shoulders, my glistening asshole open for the taking. My face burned as he lined himself up. My breath was ragged with fear.

"Not another word unless you are moaning for me," he said.

"Wait!"

My mouth clenched shut.

"*In*," he ordered. The cock struck, stretching me instantly and burrowing itself in my tight hole. I yelped through clenched teeth. It stung as it stretched me wide, making my heart nearly jump out of my chest. He wasn't gentle or slow, but I was wet, and it glided in quickly.

I was grunting from the pain, which oddly also felt insanely good. It was overwhelming and uncomfortable. Once most of his sentient cock was inside my ass, Bane released it from his grip. It came alive, coiling slowly and waiting for permission. He smiled down at it as he held onto my waist and thrust in deeper.

"Take her," he commanded.

Take her? My eyes clenched shut, and panic filled me. It began thrashing and thrusting. My face soured with the overwhelming feelings of pleasure and pain. I let out a shallow breath, crying out eagerly. Bane groaned in pleasure, tilting his head back as it moved with a mind of its own. He pulled my waist toward him and spread my cheeks with his thumbs, offering my ass to the beast. His hips swayed side to side, then jerked forward and back with its rapid movement, making my hips move in kind. His heavy first cock rested over my belly.

"Sss, that's it. Nice and deep in her tight little ass. Get what you need," he groaned, digging his fingertips into my hip. "Oh fuck, that is so good." His voice shook. The sound of his moan made my cheeks heat.

The cock twisted inside me, coiling like a corkscrew, excited by my warmth and trying to burrow deeper. I couldn't stop moaning and panting like some pornstar getting wrecked. I saw my abdomen move in waves as it thrashed. The length was getting longer and thicker, and my tight hole burned.

I tried to dig my heels into Bane's shoulders as he held me. My feet barely moved, but he still noticed. He rubbed soothing circles into my hip to calm me, resting his cheek on my calf and letting his breath cool my flushed skin as he groaned. I wanted to take it for him, so I stopped yelping and tried to relax.

"Good girl. That's it."

He grazed a thumb over my clit, rubbing it. With his other hand, he sunk four fingers in my pussy, determined to stretch me. I hollered, unable to take it all at once. He pumped them inside me forcefully, and my orgasm quickly approached. I thought I might pee. *Oh God, no. Please don't let me pee.*

"Will you bleed for me?" he growled.

"Yes!" I exclaimed as pleasure exploded through my body. I was yelling in ecstasy constantly as his second cock ravaged my ass, swaying and bouncing my hips. I repeated it over and over. I would give him anything. My pussy was squirting with cum, coating his fingers.

When my orgasm finally passed, I felt on the verge of another. Bane smiled at me again, and my heart fluttered.

"You take this so good for me," he said through rapid breaths, his veins popping in his forearms as he plunged his fingers deeper. He withdrew them and grabbed my hands, wrapping them around his girthy first cock. I could barely touch my fingers. He guided it to my entrance and pushed while making me stroke it. He stretched me until it burned. I thought my skin would tear, but he stopped. He rubbed his thumb along my entrance.

"Don't stop," he demanded.

I rubbed him, moaning loudly as he pulled at my wet entrance, massaging the skin to help it open wider. My hips jerked violently as his second cock bucked hard. I could see it moving in waves across my belly again.

Bane grabbed my hip to hold me still, then bit his lip and smiled.

"He's having so much fun in your tight little ass."

I took deep breaths to work through the shock of my tight hole being fucked wildly by his sentient cock, and my pussy being stretched by the tip of his other. He growled in satisfaction.

"Will you *bleed* for me? Will you *break* for me?" he asked excitedly as I stroked him faster, and he pressed the tip firmly against my entrance again.

"Yes! I will bleed and break. Yes! I'll give you anything," I promised.

His second cock undulated in serpentine motions, twisting and rolling more rapidly. My breath couldn't keep up, and I became dizzy, cumming again. I let out long, wailing moans and begged him to tear me open as I pumped my hands up and down his shaft.

"Fuck me. Tear me! Fuck me! Please! Now!" I yelled desperately, tears rolling down my cheeks. My brow pebbled with sweat.

Growling loudly, he pushed, and it inched past my lips, burning my entrance as it attempted to stretch around him. "You are mine. *Mine!*" he said through his pleasure, inching closer to his climax. "Will you open your body for me? Break for me? Bleed for me?"

"Yes! Yes!" I screamed as his cock wrestled its way deeper into my ass, vibrating and pounding my walls. He nudged my pussy harder, and it ached as it made slight progress. A searing, hot pain tore through my entrance as he slipped in just a little. I massaged his length faster.

"Sss. He is almost done with you. Lay still and let him finish," he said, wrapping his large hands around my waist and pushing me down. My hands dropped. He forced me to lay still as the sentient cock coiled and snaked inside me. The demon tucked his chin and panted while I screamed his name.

"Bane, *fuck* me!"

He roared, drunk on my demands. He stayed still, pushing forward slowly and allowing his second cock to exhaust itself. I had never seen such an intimidating man lose himself in such a way. He seemed almost vulnerable, trying to keep it together. He grabbed his large first cock, the head still pressed firmly against my entrance, stroking it quickly. His massive hands kept it trained against me.

"Yes, tear me open!" I begged.

He growled and squirted hot cum into my sore pussy. It was not a short climax. He pushed hard, ripping me again, but not enough to fit. My asshole felt cold and flooded. I couldn't contain the massive load; it leaked out of me as the thrashing became lazy and pulse-like. I laid still as he satisfied himself with my body for a long minute.

When he was through, his second cock purred inside me. Bane pulled it from my ass, and I watched it fall limp behind his larger one. It dripped with thick shimmering cum and flinched with exhausted pleasure, rubbing against his thigh, thankful.

Liquid leaked out of my ass. My pussy was overflowing with his cum, too, and he fingered it back into me. He lowered himself to his elbows and kissed me slowly as he pushed his spend deeper.

"You will be able to take me soon. It will hurt getting you there, but it is easier this way. Leave your water in the moonlight and drink it. Do as I say, my little dream, and we will be together soon," he reassured, catching his breath between words, and leaning down to kiss me.

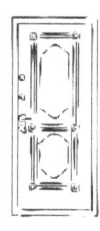

"Or you'll kill me?"

"*Kill you?*"

"If I don't... Are you going to kill me if I don't?"

He pulled his fingers from my pussy and brought them to my mouth. Our combined pleasure tasted like metal and honey.

"If you do not, you *could* die. Not because I would ever kill you but because you belong here, and your body will not survive the transition in the human world. You belong with me. You have offered yourself to me. There is no turning back."

I shivered. He could have mentioned this was a life-or-death choice before mounting me.

"You forced me. You kept me awake for days and forced me to give myself to you."

His nostrils flared, and he arched a brow.

"I asked you if you offered yourself to me, and what did you say?" he asked, grabbing my chin and tilting his head. "I asked if you would bleed and break for me, and what did you say?"

I turned my chin from his fingers. "It doesn't count in the heat of the moment. You can't just make me feel amazing and ask me life-changing questions. What about school? What about my life? I have... dreams."

He laughed low as if he had read my mind. It was like he knew I was reminding myself how much I hated going to school or the idea of having to "*people*" every day as a professional. He said nothing; he just looked down at me, smiling.

"If I do what you say, what happens then?"

"I mark you. Then, we will rule the Dream World. You will always be mine. You will sleep peacefully as often as you want, and I will give you anything, of course."

"What if I don't... What if—?" I panted, still leaking his massive load from my ass.

He tugged on my clear, gauged plugs and grinned. They burned hot, and I hissed.

"You can not escape me, my little dream. Nor do you want to."

He was right. I didn't ever want to stop looking at him or being near him. I knew it was reckless and that I should hate him for coercing me, but I made the choice to be his when I dropped my towel. Sleep deprivation was merely an excuse to do something I was ashamed to want deep down. *What have I submitted to? I should be terrified.*

"But...."

"But?" He furrowed his brows and hardened his face, reminding me of what he was. "I forget sometimes that you do not know me the way I know you. I have seen you in every dream and have craved you between every sleep. I have waited my entire life to haunt you." He stroked my lip. "You could not possibly know how deeply I feel. So tell me you do not want this, and I will leave you alone forever. You can break this off now. But say nothing, and you are mine."

My eyes darted back and forth, and my breath hitched. The idea of never seeing him again made my stomach feel painfully hollow. Something felt right with him—terrifying but right. My fists clenched.

He bit his lip, smiling wryly. "I am going to hurt you now, Buffy.

I need you to trust me. It is easier for you this way. And the sooner it is done, the sooner I can protect you."

I stiffened at his promise of pain, but when I looked into the blue swimming in the blacks of his eyes, they sparkled with sincerity. He looked at my lips as he tugged them down with his thumb and smirked. "Will you let me hurt you tonight?"

I swallowed hard, heat rushing to my cheeks. Nervous arousal swelled in my belly. I didn't know why I loved the sound of him preparing me for physical torture. Maybe it was because of how hurried he was to protect and possess me. Whatever the reason, there I was, nodding as I stared up at him, doe-eyed.

"Good girl," he whispered in his low rumble as he lowered his lips to mine.

He kissed me again, his tongue sliding against mine. Butterflies fluttered in my stomach. He took my bottom lip into his mouth, my entire bottom lip, and bit down hard. His sharp canines punctured clean through my skin. I screamed, but he wouldn't release me.

Chin-to-chin, my lower lip captured in his fangs, he seemed to groan with pleasure. Blood coated my tongue and dripped down to my jaw. His fingers gripped the top of my ears. Without warning, he stabbed his sharp thumb claws through the cartilage and slid it up, slicing both ears upward from the pinna to the helix. I screamed louder. He did it again, starting from the same spot and slicing up and out this time. A thin, triangular wedge of cartilage and skin fell from the tops of my ears. He pinched the two sides together and squeezed. The wound edges burned hot, and tears fell from my eyes as I cried. Still, I couldn't move as he mutilated me. My heart raced.

Finally, he released his fangs, his lips still practically against mine as he spoke. "Your body is going to change. It will hurt less if I do these parts for you. Do not fight me, my love."

Then he kissed me gently. The only movement I could make was to whimper. He wiped the tears from my cheek as he traced kisses along my blood-soaked jaw.

"Shhh, my little dream. You are doing so good for me. Do you need a break?"

He reached a salty tear, licking it up with his long, forked tongue. He pressed his lips to mine again, massaging my breasts in his hand.

"Stop," I pleaded, testing his word. Would he really let me take a break from the pain? My ears stung, and my punctured lip throbbed. He licked my lip and ears until they stopped bleeding. Then he kissed me until I stopped crying. The pain was gone. All that was left was his tender touch.

"You are safe, my little dream," he whispered between sweet pecks. "You are mine now. I have you." He pulled flowers from the vines around us, running them up and down my body. I melted into him after a half hour of his gentle tongue and lips caressing me. Then, while questioning my own sanity, I kissed him back.

I liked him. As bizarre as it sounded, I knew I'd think about him until the day I died. I didn't want his gentle torture to end. He wanted me and had spent hours and days making me his. It was, in a very sick way, romantic how much time he spent tormenting or pleasuring me. I was living the most fucked fairytale ever to exist, and I loved it.

"Do you still want this?" he whispered. As he kissed behind my ear lobe, I moaned, nodding my head. *Yes.* I did.

"Say it. You are well rested now, and there is no coercion. Say it and mean it. Offer yourself to me."

"I want this. I want you."

"And?"

"I'll bleed for you and break for you," I pledged, pulling his face to mine and kissing him. The pain wasn't so bad. Whatever he wanted me to do, I could handle it. Fresh blood trickled down my chin.

"Good. Let me finish. You will wake soon." He turned me onto my stomach and lifted my head by my hair. "Stick out your tongue," he instructed with a silver knife grazing my cheek. It had a thin blade no wider than a chopstick, but it was as sharp as a razor. I trembled and panted, trying to stay calm. Taunting with violence was such a strange way of seducing me, but it worked.

Shaking, I presented my tongue to him. He grabbed the tip and pulled up. He traced the blade on the underside of my tongue.

"Do you trust me?"

A tear fell from my eye, my body vibrating in fear, but I nodded. Quickly, Bane sliced the blade through the frenulum under my tongue. It stung, but it wasn't too bad. My tongue stretched out of my mouth farther as he tugged it against the ground.

"This will only hurt for a moment," he warned, stabbing the dagger clean through the tip. The end of his blade stayed wedged deep in the sand. I gasped. I was pinned to the ground with my tongue skewered.

He moaned excitedly, "Oh fuck, you did so good. We are almost done."

I breathed rapidly as he trailed his tongue down my back, biting me deeply over every ridge of my spine. His fangs ground against my bone, notching every other vertebra. I squealed in pain, my breath fogging the blade. As his fangs released from my flesh, hot blood trailed down my sides and stained the sand. The wounds stung, but I tried to force myself to stay still and calm.

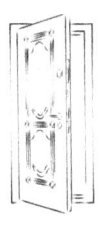

When he got to my ass, he licked it deep. I huffed out a harsh breath as my heart pounded.

"Sss, fuck. I can feel it," he groaned, eating my ass. My cheeks muffled his words. "Panic harder."

Panic harder? He loves my fear. He can feel my fear... Suddenly, it all made sense.

My cheeks burned with the praise, and I allowed myself to become consumed by my worst fears. If there was one thing I had a plethora of, it was fear and angst. I had no problem spiraling into the darkest part of my mind. I did it all the time.

Bane groaned loudly in pleasure, shoving his face deeper between my cheeks. "Good girl."

I was fully aware of how fucked this was, but I was addicted to his torture. "I will never get enough of this," he said.

Suddenly, his tongue was inside my ass. I began panting as he reached under me and rubbed my clit. I didn't think I could possibly cum again, especially not while my tongue was pinned to the ground with a blade. But the feeling of his icy cold tongue licking inside my sore ass felt incredible. He sucked and licked, and I moaned for him, my eyes rolling back as my breath fogged the silver blade. He massaged my little bundle faster and tongue-fucked my ass deeper. My body wanted to cum again, but he stopped before I could.

Instead, he crawled over me on all fours.

"Sss, look at you." Bane grabbed his second cock, stroking it. It purred and coiled awake. It was still groggy but perked up when it noticed I was slick between my cheeks.

"Hold still. I'm taking her ass this time." My heart raced, hoping Bane would be gentle so my tongue didn't rip through the blade. His cock held as still as it could, vibrating with excitement as it complied.

"Let me see how well you can behave," he said, unfreezing me. I could have ripped the knife out and stabbed him if I wanted. This was my chance. I could crawl away and try to wake myself. But I didn't. I raised my ass, getting on my knees and forearms. Eagerness grew in him.

He pressed the tip against my asshole and pushed it inside, moaning. He was gentle and slowly plunged it deep, pumping it into me a little harder. The blade sliced my tongue little by little with each thrust.

"Go deeper," he demanded of his cock. It grew, vibrating in excitement. He moaned, fucking my ass slowly for a long while, rubbing my clit and resting his large cock on my lower back.

"Can you take more?" His thrusting was slow and deep as he rubbed my back, loosening my muscles and using my blood to break the friction between his hands and my skin. With my tongue still pinned to the ground, all I could do was make the closest sound to "yes." He picked up the pace, hissing at my consent.

I came for him, moaning and clawing at the sand. My cheeks were hot, my head was light, and my ass was burning and sore. He let out a breath of excitement, hearing me come undone.

"I will never get over seeing you like this," he said as he fucked my ass faster and harder. My pleasure was spent. I couldn't cum anymore, so I laid still for him, letting him take my ass for as long as he wanted. He had no need to paralyze me. I would let him tear me open from tongue to ass. Drool spilled from the side of my mouth as he railed me. He stroked his larger cock as he chased relief.

My body rocked, and my tongue tugged against the blade, slicing a little more. My heart pounded, and I gasped at the pain. The sound drove Bane over the edge. Finally, he came inside me again. The release took a while, and he growled loudly. I stayed still while he finished, and a moan escaped my lips at the feeling of his chilled cum filling me and dripping down my back, mixing with the blood still dripping from his bite marks. He panted, leaving his purring cock inside for a long moment after. I was his good girl, his little slut. I loved it.

"Lay flat," Bane huffed. He laid on top of me as I complied, leaning down and grabbing the handle of the dagger. His spirited cock rested inside me, satisfied and nuzzling the walls of my ass affectionately as it softened. Bane kissed my shoulders up to my neck, cold breath ricocheting off my skin.

"Are you ready, my little dream?" he whispered between pants.

I nodded. Without hesitation, he sliced the tip of my tongue clean through the center. I could feel his cock shudder in excitement inside my ass. Like his, my tongue was now forked about an inch deep. Blood dripped from my mouth, down my chin, and into the sand.

He dropped his weight on top of me and kissed every inch of my neck and between my shoulders again. He was sweaty and cold and panting against me.

"The worst is yet to come, my love. But soon, I will have you and mark you as mine," he said, gripping my hair. "You are my everything. Do as I say, and I can have you forever."

"Okay."

"Okay, what?" he said, reaching under me and hugging me tightly. His chest fought for space against my back as he caught his breath. He nipped at my ear and thrusted his hips hard. "Say my name, baby."

"Bane," I moaned with a bloody smile.

Only I had woken up moaning his name. Light was shining on my eyelids, and I opened them.

I was soaked and leaking cum from my ass. Panting, I turned my head to see Neveah looking at me in disgust. Not even her neon pink arm cast and now bedazzled sling could distract me from the face she was making. She threw her Bedazzler on the desk.

"So now you're having wet dreams about the demon you hate so much?"

"What?"

Neveah stood up, grabbed her Razer phone, and gave me a thorough dose of side-eye. As she walked out of the room, she mockingly moaned, "Oh Bane, oh *Bane*. I just *love* your demon cock."

The taste of blood coated my tongue. I looked at my water bottle on the window ledge and grabbed it. As I took a swig of the metallic water, something hard hit the edge. I touched my lips. Where he had bitten me was hard. Naked, I rushed to the mirror, clutching my blanket to my chest.

Small silver spikes were threaded where his fangs had pierced through. They were like his but smaller. My teeth were stained with blood. My ears, with a line of fleshy red wounds, were now pointed like his. The gauged earrings were bigger now and made of crystals. My tongue, still raw and slowly bleeding, was long, thick and forked like his. I rolled it out of my mouth and watched it flick well past my chin, flexing both tips to cross over each other. He was carving me into his queen, little by little.

Still thirsty for the metallic water, I chugged it quickly, looking at my bed, covered in flowers.

9

BANE

Buffy disappeared from under me, but this time I smiled. I picked up the pieces of cartilage and kept them tight in my fist. They disappeared, landing in my study for safekeeping.

The sand was stained with her blood. I sat on my heels, scooping up every crimson grain. I cupped the bloody pile hard in my palms, heating and crushing it until two large red crystals formed. I smiled; I would carve them into two new gauges, polish them, set them in silver rings, and gift them to her when she bore my children. I held them tight in my grip, and like the cartilage, they disappeared.

I stood up, the sand falling away from my skin easily. With a relieved sigh, I slowly walked back to the main cavern. My chest was puffed out, my chin held high, and my shoulders set back. The wind tasted crisper, and the lapping water sounded more rhythmic.

I picked a morning glory from a vine and smelled it. Unlike the morning glories in her world, these had a potent smell that electrified your senses. I wondered how many I would have to squeeze dry to make her a perfumed oil. She would have anything she wanted—my little dream.

I picked hundreds along the beach on my way back, squeezing them in my palm until they landed in safekeeping. I would gift her the oil for her marking. Somehow, every other gift I could think of didn't seem like enough.

She was falling for me. I felt it. Her heart had leapt for me in the showers. She submitted to me quickly. She offered her body to me when I skewered her tongue into the sand. I could feel it in her. She was more than infatuated. She adored me almost as much as I did her.

As I approached the main cavern, Slater and his squad of demons were huddled by the opening. The filches stood behind them, waiting for their assignments. They were once sleep demons but over-indulged in the human world and ran out of energy. Taking more than they gave, they were bound to the Dream World, never to travel to other worlds again. Powerless and weak, they dwelled in the bubbling waters, feeding off what tiny creatures they could still terrify. Their skin was a sickly gray with a coat of slime, and their black hair was thinned to a scraggly few that clung to bald heads. The spirit in their sentient cocks had abandoned them, leaving behind shriveled skin that hung behind their flaccid larger cocks.

The group turned to me; the filches fell to both knees while Slater and his men dropped to one before rising slowly. Slater approached first.

"*Your Grace*," he said, keeping formalities in the presence of his squads. He smirked at my relaxed demeanor. "You look well tended to."

"She is almost ready. She did so well," I stated with pride. I was not inflating the facts to garner trust in their future queen. Buffy indeed did incredible with her transitions so far. Fear, pain, and pleasure had flooded her tonight. I could feel all of it. The only thing she did not feel was misery—the only emotion I could not stand to feed off of. I could handle her anger, exhaustion, and despair as I tortured her, keeping her from her rest. But misery? If I felt that in her, I'm not sure I would be able to stomach it, and whoever was the culprit would suffer. That quickly made me recall some unfinished business. "Where is the prisoner?"

Slater smiled, the hollow silver piercings in his lower lip clinking against his teeth. He turned, nodding at two of his demons.

"Get the dweeb," he ordered. The two demons charged over the dunes, past the entrance to a cave farther back designated for prisoners before we sentenced them.

"The filches are weak out of water. They are away from their only energy source. We need to think about how to sustain them," Slater counseled.

"I have already accounted for that."

He nodded, standing beside me as we looked out over the bubbling water. "How long before she is marked?"

"Perhaps next time I see her. She needs rest. The coming days will be hard for her."

"Should you not be with her then?"

"I would give her no rest. I will stay here and get things ready for her. This will be a very different life than she had planned. I have to make it comfortable."

"What do you have in mind?"

"For her? I will give her the crystal moon."

He nodded, glancing over at me. "What is it like? Burying yourself in your dream?" Slater asked, a sadness in his voice. Although sleep demons dreamt of one person their entire life, it was never guaranteed that they would find them—especially if that person were a human, like ours. It was reasonable that he would be envious.

"*Love*, you mean? What does love feel like? Better than all of the terror in the world. Indescribable. Unconditional," I said, turning toward the dunes as the sounds of groaning and sobs grew near. My eyes darkened, lip twitching. "And violently protective."

The two demons returned, dragging a thin, naked human. Blood ran down his legs. "Ple... please. Let me go." The human's once-tall black spikes of hair fell flat, and eyeliner dripped down his face. The demons threw him at my feet.

Hushed whispers buzzed around the filch group; we never dragged humans to the Dream World for reasons other than pairing or marking. But the prisoner was clearly here for neither, oozing with misery and pain. The filches, hungry for the human terror they had not tasted in years, shoved their way to the front to get a better look.

"*Skeeter*, is it?" I questioned, looking down at the pitiful human. He looked up at me, trembling.

"Listen, man, I... I don't know what I did, but I'll give you anything. Please, just let me go."

"Anything? Anything I want?"

"Yes! I swear, dude! You name it. I have connections, okay?"

"What do you know of Buffy?"

The skeevy little human huffed out a laugh, old blood still caked in his teeth. "*Buffy*? Sure, man. You want Buffy? Have her. I'll bait her for you. She's a stuck-up little bitch, though. Just warning you. And, like, she totally plays dead fish in bed, too. Unless you're like...

you're going to *kill* her?" He shifted his eyes around the group nervously. Blood trickled from his ass, which was still ripped open from being sodomized with a phallic-shaped stone. "Fuck it. She's a bitch anyway. I'll get her for you. I'll rape or kill her *for* you, dude. Whatever. Shit. Just let me go, man. Please."

My heart raced with rage. My lips twitched again. I paralyzed him, making his bloody body fall to the sand.

"As you all know, we must find the Sandman before the Samhain. But walking out of the water will make you tired and weak. Here, I have a human who has vowed to defile and assassinate your future queen. The penalty is death."

The human's eyes widened, and he panted, screaming through clenched teeth. I let his fear radiate to the filches, like the scent of a hog on a spit dancing under the noses of starved men. They growled and licked their slimy jowls.

"However, that would be wasteful given the opportunity this brings us. I give you one hour to get your fill of him, but he must be kept alive. Fill your energy. Then, search every last inch of this world. The first filch who brings me a valuable lead, leading to the capture of the Sandman, will have this human as their prize, to do with what they want for as long as he lives."

They stepped forward, swarming the puny human like flies to a slab of meat. I released him, freeing his muscles. He scrambled to his knees, screaming, and tried to get away. But they grabbed him, holding him down by each limb.

"And while hunting for the Sandman, harvest every feathered dandelion you can find. I will only let your new queen sleep in the softest bed." I walked away as they began their torment, taking turns feeding off of his terror and filling their bulbs with seed for the first time since becoming a damned filch. This couldn't reverse their cursed fate, but they felt like sleep demons for the first time in years.

Slater nodded for his squad of demons to stay behind to ensure the filches didn't kill the human. Then he followed me to the main cavern, where we descended into the darkness.

"And all these years, I thought I was the ruthless one," he commented, looking back at the feast of horror. "What does it mean to 'play dead fish in bed?'"

"It means he does not know a thing about pleasuring a woman. None will miss him."

"I do not even prefer women, and I know where a fucking clit is. How is that possible?"

"It is a level of pathetic I have never understood—"

"Your grace!" Overton called, running toward me and kneeling too quickly. His knee barely grazed the floor. It was all I could do not to strip his rank and have him kneeling on both knees like a commoner. It made my already thin patience with him fragile.

"Yes, Overton?"

"Is it true? You dragged a human to the Dream World for the filches to torture? This is unheard of! You are breaking several rules. It *cannot* be carried out. You *must* return him."

"Slater, Overton is relieved of his duty for the next three days and is in your care to learn some *fucking* respect," I snarled. Overtons face drew back, expecting to reason with me or coax a scare from me. I walked away. His misery was palpable, and I scuffed in disgust. The taste of despair was revolting.

Slater grabbed him by the back of the neck hard, startling him. "There is a cage under my bed. Go lay in it, *slumdog*," Slater demanded with a smile as he pushed Overton to the ground. "And crawl there."

I swung open my study doors. Khadijah was at my desk, tracing her fingers over the pieces of Buffy's ears that I carved off. Nerebye was everything else I sent for safekeeping.

"I take it you did not go slow, as I advised?" she said. I walked over to her and took the cartridge from her thin hands. The pieces were still warm. I brushed the sand off, kissed them slowly, and placed them next to the jar of morning glories I had picked and the red crystals I made from the bloody sand.

"She handled it well. She has started breaking. It's like she was made for this pain."

"You burden her with too much at once."

"I will not touch her again for a few nights. I'll be getting our new room ready."

"She will need extra healing. I will have my students join the chants for her when she sleeps."

"You are invaluable, Khadijah. Thank you. Please send her pleasant dreams. Let her rest well and easily. Warm her pillow, too, but not too much. She does not like her bed hot. And—"

"Of course. We will do all of that in our chants for her," Khadijah reassured, fingering through my collection of Buffy's things again. "So... you *will* stay away from her? You have only had a taste. You will not be able to hold back for long, and she will pull your energy right out of you. The people will not stand to have a filch king who murdered his queen."

"I have more than enough restraint to avoid becoming a damned filch, and I would never let anything happen to her! You *insult* me."

"Forgive me. Love is a new emotion for you. It can be blinding. I only wish to help. It is our world's interest I have in mind, as well as *yours*, old friend."

"Of course," I said, grabbing a blood crystal and shaving it into a cylinder with my dagger. "Is there anything else?"

Khadijah paused, tapping her nailless fingers on my desk. Finally, she cleared her throat. "Did you tell her? Does she know what will happen to her next?"

I sighed, looking around at the images of her face swirling in luminous smoke. The transition would be cruel and unrelenting, but I had no doubt in my mind that she could handle it.

"There is no sense in instilling that level of terror if I cannot be with her to help."

10

BUFFY

I hadn't heard from Bane in three nights. I slept well but was tired often, and my body hurt badly. I did what he asked. I left my water in the moonlight and drank it every morning, using more than one bottle. I was incredibly thirsty for the metallic taste, and it seemed to soothe the pain. Even in autumn, it was hot here, but the water was still ice cold no matter how long it sat out in the sun. By the second night, I had three bottles on the windowsill and six bottles by night three. I knew it was laced with something, but I didn't care. He told me to do it. It was that simple. I was completely consumed by him. I trusted him.

I needed to see Bane again. I needed him to take me. I slept naked every night, waiting for his touch. When he didn't come, I touched myself. But it was too much to bear as splitting pain shot through my core. The skin on my center was tender and achy. I took a swig of water to dull the aches and surprisingly fell asleep with ease, my pillow soft and warm.

My dreams were pleasant memories from my past. But when I woke up refreshed, not sleep-deprived or haunted, and I realized he hadn't pulled me to the Dream World, my stomach would twist in knots. Why hadn't he visited? Why was I dreaming so nicely? He hadn't even sent me a nightmare to show he was thinking of me. He hadn't crept in the shadows or made the room too cold again to show me he cared.

The shooting pain would start again as soon as I woke. It was worse in the morning and increased every day like my body was splitting in two. He told me it would hurt, but I thought he would be here to ease the stress of it.

As I packed for the break, I looked at the space under Neveah's bed where she usually kept the Ouija box and thought about calling him. That was the rule after a good date, wasn't it? You wait three days to call, so you don't seem desperate? Maybe he was waiting three days to call? Maybe he was bored of me. My heart twisted at the thought.

It was no use denying it now; I had feelings for my sleep-paralysis demon. More than that, I had an unhealthy obsession with him. I swung my bag over my shoulder and left the room, glancing at the dark space under her bed one more time.

Halloween Break was here, and I was heading home to visit my parents and wondered if he would be able to find me. I squinted at the sun; it was blinding. I scrambled for my sunglasses, but they barely helped. When I got to my car, a police officer stopped me.

"Ms. Fatone?"

"Yes…" I said, brushing hair from my face.

"Officer Norris. Where are you heading?" he asked, getting out of the passenger side of an unmarked cruiser. He flashed his badge.

"Back home... for Halloween Break."

"Since when do colleges give students a Halloween Break?"

"Since the student council voted to swap it out with Spring Break since the summer runs long most of the year here, and we never see the seasons change? Since Halloween Horror Nights got Alien Assault. Since... I don't know. I'm sorry. Can I help you with something?"

"Are you familiar with Fred Mosquito Valentine?"

"What the hell kind of name is that? No. I have no idea who that is."

"He went by Skeeter. Does this photo ring a bell?" He held out a senior picture of the guy in question.

A cramp ripped through my core, and I clutched my belly. "Ah... yeah. Skeeter. I know him. I heard he's missing."

"When was the last time you saw him?"

"Umm." I tried to count back the days, wincing at the pain. My forehead beaded with sweat, and I reached for my water. The cop tensed, grabbing at his holstered weapon. I slowly finished pulling the water out of my bag, wide-eyed. "A few days ago. What's going on?" I unscrewed the cap, taking a swig.

"What day?"

I shrugged. "Five days ago, I think? Monday maybe? Why?"

"And what was the nature of your interaction?"

"I hadn't slept well and felt sick, so he walked me back to my dorm and left."

"Any altercation?"

"What? No... I mean, he tried to hook up, and I told him no. But he left, and that was it."

"What time was that?"

"Late. I don't know! Eleven PM? Have you guys really not found him?"

"Ms. Fatone, we have witnesses who say you were one of the last to be seen with him alive."

"*Alive?*"

"Where are you going exactly? Can we have an address?"

"My mother's house. Umm, here." I gave them my state ID. "I never changed the address."

He took a photo of the card and started copying down my information. I cringed at the pain again and leaned forward slightly.

"Is something wrong?"

"Period cramps. I'll be fine."

He arched a brow and handed the ID back with his business card tucked between his first fingers. "If you hear anything, give me a call. I'll be in touch."

I narrowed my eyes at him and reached for my door. As soon as I sat in the car, I swallowed hard and darted my eyes back and forth. Could Bane have killed Skeeter? My cheeks prickled with heat, and I smiled softly at the thought. Stimming, I tugged on the spike he pierced into my lip. I pushed the sharp end into my fingertip and let out a short laugh.

Did he kill just for me? Did he torture him for touching me? Would he kill anyone who hurt me? In the back of my head, the old me screamed at how sick I was for loving the thought. But the old me was quickly dying, carved out with my ears. I could feel my blood turning cold in my veins as my heart swelled with pride. Even my center heated at the thought. Bane must have taken Skeeter out for trying to take what was his, and all I could do was blush like a giddy teen.

CHAIN MAIL

I had been driving for hours when the cramps hit again. I pulled over. They had only gotten worse since leaving the school, and my bones seemed to be cracking, no, snapping. My hips, center, spine, and even my jaw felt as though they had been broken in half. I rested my head on my steering wheel and breathed through it. My palms were slick with sweat, and I dug gashes into my steering wheel with my nails. I screamed and arched my back, bouncing off of my seat in pain. Then I looked down and noticed I was bleeding through my pants.

"Shit..."

I had lied to the cop. I wasn't due for my period, and I panicked as the blood saturated my jeans from front to back. I drove quickly to my parents' house, only a few more miles away. I screamed in pain all the way to their driveway, chugging a bottle and a half of moon-charged water until the pain all but stopped.

When I arrived, I clutched my last water bottle and got out of the car, shaking. I nearly threw the damn thing. I had done everything Bane had asked, and he left me in pain, waiting for him, pining over him. I didn't deserve this. I needed to summon him *now*.

No one was home, so I ran to the phone and dialed Neveah's number. She picked up on the first ring.

"Hello?"

"Hey, it's Buffy."

"What up, biatch? Hurry up; I'm about to leave for Tennessee."

I rolled my eyes. "Hey, um... is there any way you can drop the Ouija board off to me at my mom's place on your way?"

Laughter burst out of the receiver, and I pulled the phone away from my ear. "You're so horny for that demon, aren't you? Well, the answer is no. I dumped that shit on Skyler days ago. She can deal with all that creepy shit and get her arm broken. Little slut."

Anger churned in my stomach. What if Bane preferred Skyler? What if that was why I hadn't seen him? My face prickled with jealousy. Tears welled in my eyes. I envisioned myself the next time I saw Skyler, choking her until she was within an inch of her life and then laughing at the fear on her face. *What the hell is wrong with me lately?*

"Neveah, I need you to get it back from her! Listen, I... I can't explain, but it's *really* important," I said as a wave of cramps returned and blood trickled down my leg.

"Chill out!" she barked. "O.M.G. You're, like, obsessed. You know that, right?"

Yes. There was no other explanation for the constant desire to see him, feel him, or try to fit him inside me. The fear, the pain, the pleasure, it was all addicting. But it was something more. I felt connected to him. I was his. I wanted him to be mine. I needed him to be mine. My hollow eyes stared off into the distance in thought, but I pulled myself back.

"Whatever. Say what you want, but promise me you'll get it back before you leave. I'll pick it up myself if I have to."

"Yeah, sure. I'll see what I can do."

The phone disconnected. I cringed as the cramps returned, but they were not nearly as bad. I gripped the counter hard and thought I might shatter the granite. My mother walked through the door, returning from visiting Dad at the nursing home. She caught me hunched over and groaning, and sprinted to me.

"Honey, what's wrong?" she cooed. When I stood up, she

recoiled. "Jesus! What happened? What did you do to your ears? Why are you blue?"

"Blue?"

"Your skin is blue! Why are the whites of your eyes so dark? And... Oh my goodness, you're bleeding, honey! We need to get you to the hospital!"

I didn't argue. The blood alone was scaring me, let alone my mother's shrieking and shaking. But then I held my hands up. I had always been pale, but my skin now had a faint bluish hue. Was I losing that much blood?

———

I sat in a hospital bed, waiting for the imaging and lab work to come back. The bleeding had stopped, but the flesh between my legs was tender and sensitive. I refused the pelvic exam, remembering how rough my gynecologist was during my pap smears. The pain medication helped the cramping a little, but I could still feel it, like a nagging ache in my bones.

Mom returned from the vending machine with two hot chocolates and some honey buns, and continued to grill me about my sudden body modifications. Somehow, saying, "You know, when I was little, I always wanted to be a fairy," didn't stop her.

"Hi there. Mom, can I ask you to step out of the room for a bit?" the doctor asked as he poked his head through the door. Offended, my mother looked back and forth between the two of us. Finally, she threw her hands up and stood, snatching up her hot chocolate and purse.

"Okay. You're an adult now, Jellybean. I get it," she said

begrudgingly, hustling her thin frame out of the room. "But so help me if you are pregnant!"

"Mom!"

She shrugged and disappeared beyond the threshold. The doctor shut the door and sat down next to my bed.

"How are you feeling, young lady?"

"Better. The cramping is gone for now. The bleeding stopped, too."

He nodded silently, waiting for me to say something. I had nothing else to say.

"Well, a few things about your tests are troubling me. Can you guess what they might be?"

I shook my head.

"We'll start with the *argyria* you're experiencing. That would be the bluish-silver color your skin is developing as a result of the high silver content in your blood."

"Silver?"

"Yes. Have you, by any chance, been drinking colloidal silver, a popular fad supplement these days?"

"Not that I know of. I drink water every day, and it tastes… normal. It's fine," I lied.

He raised his brows. "Perhaps it has something to do with your pelvis? Have you had any surgeries outside the country lately that you forgot to mention?"

"What? No… *why?*" I shook my head.

"Your pelvis has been broken in three places, and between the fracture lines is a build-up of some type of metal. I think it may be silver. It caused your pelvis to widen a significant amount. Does that ring a bell?"

"Why on earth would I have silver—?"

"Another body modification, I assumed. I see you did quite a number on your ears and tongue. Not to mention the darkening of your sclerae, which I assume is from the *first* tattoo session. Now, God knows what you did to elongate your pupils. I've never seen them stretch to that shape, but I'll bet it's contributing to your photosensitivity," he rambled, shining a penlight into my eyes without warning. I looked at him sideways. "And then there are the metal growths on your *spine*."

"Metal growths on my spine?"

"Spikes, it appears... under the skin for now, although they look sharp and are causing pressure ulcers to form on your skin. They will pop through if they aren't shaved down or removed. Ms. Fatone, if you want to mutilate your body, that is your choice, but it will come with dangerous and undesirable side effects."

Anger crawled through my chest. All I could think about was making him shut up. He grabbed his throat momentarily as if he was having trouble breathing. He looked terrified and his chest had stopped rising and falling. It was almost as if I could feel how nervous it made him, and it gave me a rush. It didn't last long.

"I'm not doing body modifications. I didn't do this to myself."

"Excuse me." He cleared his throat and loosened his tie. "I recommend a follow-up with your gynecologist about the bleeding. Unless you consent to a pelvic examination here, there is nothing more I can do for you on that front. Your blood cultures are negative, so you're not septic. That's a wonder in itself, especially with the spinal work. I'll send you home with a prescription for tramadol for the pain and a strong recommendation to avoid heavy metals. The blue tint to your skin is likely permanent and will worsen if you further expose yourself to silver. An orthopedic doctor should examine the metal bone graphing immediately, so I'll refer you to one. But! None of this is an emergency, so there is no reason to keep you overnight. Please do avoid the sketchy black market body modification doctors. They're often unlicensed for an excellent reason." He got up and turned away, heading for the door.

My jaw went slack. I was angry but too confused to do anything but snap, "You know, your bedside manner really *sucks*."

He nodded, unphased. Smacking his lips, he said, "Have a nice day, Ms. Fatone. The nurse will be in with your discharge paperwork shortly."

Livid and wanting answers immediately, I was determined to get a hold of Bane that night, no matter what.

11

BUFFY

After dinner with my mother, I convinced her to stop at the mall. I was able to slip away for a moment and go into a lingerie store to find something lacy and blue. I found a skimpy bra and panty set with transparent lace that seemed to shine when the light caught it. *He'll love it. He'll never disappear on me again.* The woman at the counter looked me up and down, disapproving of my strange appearance. Abashedly, I paid and shoved the garments to the bottom of my cross-body purse.

Then I hurried into Spender's Gifts. I couldn't wait for Neveah to *maybe* bring me the board. The shop's back wall was always full of the most perverse merchandise. Halloween was the next day, and they had a massive inventory of spooky things on sale, including cheap Ouija boards. I grabbed one from the top of the stack and checked out, hoping the double bag would hide it from my mother.

I had no such luck. As soon as I left the store, she walked over to me, eyeing the large package. She nudged it open and peeked in, only to recoil.

"It's a gag gift for my roommate."

"Well, don't use it. You'll get some demon haunting you," Mom said. That was the hope.

"What did you get?" I asked, looking at her small bag. She lifted it with a smile and handed it to me.

"Oh, this? This is so I can keep better tabs on you and make sure you're not bleeding out somewhere or getting a finger removed."

"No way! A razer?" I hugged her, ignoring the nauseating pain ripping through my stomach or the way her arms hit my tender spine. It wasn't lost on me that the chain mail the other week said I would get a new phone *and* a new love interest.

But I was growing tired. Luckily, Mom was just as thrilled to get home as I was. On the ride back, I set up my new flip phone, texting Harvey first. I texted Neveah next, who said she'd left the board on my bed in the dorm.

When I was finally alone in my childhood room while the world slept and the clock ticked closer to midnight, I lit a candle and opened the board impatiently. It was nothing like Bane's. This one had a flimsy cardboard base and a plastic mouse with a cheap acrylic window. I undressed for him, sat on my floor in my new lingerie, and took a deep breath. I went to reach for the mouse but stopped.

I hadn't combed my hair or shaved my legs yet. I didn't know if it mattered to Bane, but I didn't want to risk looking like some scrub and scaring him off. As far as demons go, he was probably out of my league.

I hurried to clean myself up, shaving with my dad's old electric shaver and spraying myself with copious amounts of Calgon

Turquoise Seas. I grabbed the strappy rhinestone studded heels from my senior prom and popped them on. Then I glided blue raspberry-flavored Lip Smackers on my lips, used the clothing iron to straighten my hair, and plucked stray hairs from my eyebrows. After one last adjustment of my chest, perking my breasts up in the sheer royal blue cups and pulling the straps of the matching thong over my hips a little higher, I was ready.

Totally overthinking it, I pressed my fingers against the mouse, closed my eyes, and spoke. "I summon Bane, the demon in my dreams." I waited. There was no cold wind or haunting feeling that someone was behind me. I felt alone. The mouse was still. "I summon Bane! The demon of the Dream World." I waited again. Nothing happened. I pulled my hands from the mouse, chewing on my cheek in embarrassment. Was this board a dud? Or did I look too desperate? I covered myself in a fluffy robe, leaning against the bed and hugging my waist.

Huffing, I touched it again, this time with one hand. "Bane?"

The mouse turned cold. I tightened my legs together as excitement rose. "Bane, I need to talk to you. Please."

The mouse moved across the board briskly, spelling out a reply.

Hello.

I smirked. "Bane, is that you?"

NO.

I furrowed my brows. "Can you get him for me? Please. I need to speak to him."

Beautiful.

I read it under my breath. I tightened my robe across my chest and cleared my throat. "Thank you. Can you please get Bane for me? He's the demon of—"

A cold breeze skated up my inner thigh. I gasped. A deep laugh passed by my ear and then faded away.

The mouse moved again. *Why?*

"That's between him and I."

Suddenly, I was slammed onto my back, and my robe was ripped open. My throat was tight. I tried to scream, but I couldn't. Invisible hands ran up my body, grabbing anywhere they could. I heard another laugh and kicked with all my strength. Finally, the pressure from above me lifted.

I turned over and scrambled to my hands and knees, crawling away. Something pulled at my robe. I wrestled my arms out, moving faster. My legs were pulled out from under me as something dragged my body under the bed. I tried to cry out and clawed the carpet, but it was useless. I was pulled under and into the floor. Darkness closed over me. I tried to scream again, calling for Bane as the world around me turned dark and hard.

The dragging feeling stopped, but a body lay on top of me. It was pitch black, and the ground was cold and stone-like. My eyes adjusted easily, and I could see I was in a musty cave. It smelled of damp wood and dust, and water lapped nearby.

"What do you know of *Bane?*" a man croaked gleefully into my ear, pulling my hair until my neck was angled back painfully. I shoved the fear away and tried to stay calm. This spirit was *not* a friend of Bane. That much was clear.

"Nothing. I've seen him in my dreams, that's all."

"Mmmm. You are lying," he said, reaching his hands under me and into my panties.

"No!" I screamed, wrestling him, and that same haunting laugh echoed around me. I screamed louder, but he pushed his fingers between my lips. I cried out as he rubbed my small bundle in circles and yanked my head back harder. I whined in agony and shame.

He licked the tip of my pointed ear. "You look awfully *slutty* tonight for just a quick chat with Bane. Tell me, has he tried to mark you yet?"

"I don't know what you're talking about," I panted.

He touched my center gently. I kicked and bucked as my body betrayed me. A tear fell from my eye. "You are soaked for him, and you *reek* of silver."

"It's a silver supplement. Stop!" There was no doubt in my mind that I hated every second of this, but his fingers knew how to make my body react. "Please stop. Please! Stop!" I screamed, clenching my thighs and trying to squirm away from his touch. He pushed me back into the cold ground harder, and I winced in pain.

He plunged deeper inside of me, his thumb rubbing my clit. "Bane!" I shrieked as the strange demon fingered me harder. "Bane!" I screamed over and over again until my voice broke.

He let go of my hair and scratched his nails down my back. He split the skin until silver spikes popped through, the skin stretching around the base of each. It felt like fire was melting my flesh away. I screamed in pain, but it did nothing to stop me from inching closer to a regretful release.

"*Silver.* So you *are* his dream, then? *I knew it.*"

"No. No! Bane!" My heart raced. I kicked and clawed at the ground, crying and screaming as the unmistakable warmth of an impending climax swelled in my belly.

He rested a palm on the small of my back. It felt as though a thousand bees were stinging my skin. I hissed in pain, and he rubbed my clit faster. Then he traced the hand from my back to my front, ripping a breast out of my bra. "No..." I whimpered, my voice hoarse from screaming. Tears trailed down my cheeks. Weak and in pain, I stopped fighting. He would make me cum. He pinched my nipple and sucked on my earlobe. "No..."

"Tell Bane..." he murmured as his fingers worked me over the edge. I sobbed as my release approached. He kicked my legs open wider. "...that the Sandman wants what is his... or I will take what is most precious to him."

I weakly moaned as pleasure burst in my core. My warmth puddled in his palm, and I buried my face into the cold ground in shame as I moaned through my sobs. He pressed my face down as he pulled his fingers from me. I lay still, confused, ashamed, and angry.

He yanked my panties to the side and shoved his length inside me. I cried out as he moaned, thrusting hard. My skin scraped against the rough stone floor. He had to slow down to stop himself from cumming too soon, drawing out the horrible experience for as long as he could. I stopped feeling sorry for myself at that moment. Tears still fell from my eyes, but I grimaced in anger. Bane would kill him for this. Even as I cringed with every thrust, I found comfort in the thought of my demon tearing him to shreds.

Just when I thought it couldn't get any worse, the pain came back, ripping through my center and down my spine like lightning and fire. I screamed, and he pushed into my painful center harder. I didn't give him the satisfaction of begging him to stop. I knew he wouldn't. I dug my nails into the dusty ground and imagined Bane inflicting the same agony on him. But my body was exhausted.

When the pain finally passed, I lay still, sobbing angrily until he was done.

"Oh, he would have loved this pussy," he taunted, pulling out. "It's a shame I can't finish inside it tonight. Maybe next time." He walked in front of me and kneeled; he grabbed a fist full of my hair and pulled me forward.

"No…" I said in a hoarse voice. But the second my mouth opened, he shoved his cock inside. He fucked my face hard. I choked and gagged, but he wouldn't let up. His pelvic bone crashed into my nose, and I heard a crack; hot fluid leaked down my chin. The Sandman didn't last long, filling my mouth with his cum. He moaned pathetically. It tasted like mud and was gritty and thick. I gagged, trying to pull away, but he nearly ripped the hair out of my head, smashing back into my mouth. Panting, he held my face against him, keeping the length deep as I choked without reprieve. His gritty skin against my tongue made me want to cut it out of my mouth.

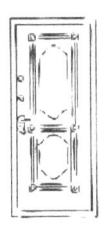

"Swallow it," he demanded. Desperate for it to be over, I complied, gagging once more. My lower back burned anew. He laughed and pulled out. I gasped for air and hacked, feeling grit come up. I heard sand hit the ground under my face with every cough.

He walked behind me as I got to my hands and knees, sniffling, crying, and gasping. I shook with anger, ready to slice him open from ear to ear.

"He has three days before you choke to death on it." With his hand still soaked from my release, he slapped my bare ass hard.

I woke up with a jolt. I was lying against my bed on the floor, wrapped in my fluffy robe, which was bloody from my newly cut spikes. The blood was matted to the fabric. My body trembled. My spine stung.

The candle was nearly spent. The cheap Ouija board was exactly how I left it. I opened the bottom of my robe to see my center wet with blood, and even more blood dripped from my face onto the carpet between my legs. Blotting my nose, I confirmed it was a nosebleed.

But the worst part was the taste of the Sandman, which was still fresh on my tongue. I coughed into my hand, and to my horror, my palm was sprinkled with sand.

12

BANE

It had been three nights. I could not bear being away from her. The dreams of her were terrible, and not in a nice way. She was clearly in pain but handled it well, drinking her water. Buffy did not look happy, though, and I was not even torturing her. That's all I could see in the too-short dreams.

When I woke, I got to work crafting gifts for her marking. I worked my fingers raw, carving her new gauges from the blood crystals and working every last drop of oil from the flowers to make her a sweet perfume. The filches scouted for the Sandman and returned with large bags full of feathered dandelion petals; I stuffed a duvet with them. Then I sweated for hours as I chipped away at the walls of our new room, polishing and crafting it. It was stunning, yet nothing I did felt like enough after the dreams of her suffering.

I waited in her dorm room, eager to feel her fear and excitement for the first time in nights. She wasn't here. I walked through the darkest shadows of the campus, only to find it deserted. I could sense her nowhere. I could not travel outside the areas where the humans had recited the chain mail spells. I was stuck here unless she used a proper summoning spell or called me by The Ivory Board, neither of which she did.

I searched her usual spots, finally landing at her guy friend's dorm. She tried to hide from me here once, but I had watched her lie awake, exhausted and terrified. I had kept her uncomfortably cold to torture her, and she looked too cute when she was desperate for warmth. I smiled, remembering how she piled comforters, fleece throws, and jackets over her until she practically buried herself in plush, yet she shivered the whole night.

She trusted this human, and he had never wronged her. He sat on his bed in his empty dorm, stroking himself behind a sports magazine. I had a feeling I knew his type, but this confirmed it. I had no reason to worry about him at all. As fun as it was to watch, she was not here, and I needed to find her.

I woke his desk box. It was like Buffy's but with sharper corners and a solid beige casing. The boy was startled when the glass side glowed bright. He stopped his stroking for a moment to glance over. But was ultimately unbothered by it.

He returned to his magazine, looking at a man garbed in a helmet, tight clothes, and padded armor. In the photo, he crouched behind another man dressed in similar attire, holding a brown, oblong ball between his legs. The boy replenished the lotion in his hand and stroked himself faster.

He was well distracted and didn't notice me sifting through the messages displayed. I found his "email address" and made a mental note. There were no messages from Buffy aside from the old ones that had been sent days before. My jaw ticked. Where the *hell* was she? I left him there, moaning and squirting on the photo of the crouching man in silly tight pants.

I checked the library. It was empty, aside from a couple of girls talking about the missing dweeb. He had apparently been rough with both of them, and I knew I had done the right thing by keeping him prisoner. He would never bother them again. He would feel karma's harsh resentment tenfold. But I grew bored and angry that I had not found my dream yet.

I sat on Buffy's bed, waiting in the darkness. Had the transition been too much? Had she run away from me after everything she went through for me? For *us*? We belonged together. I clenched my fist. She was mine. *I will hunt her down and torture her until I have proven my love is—*.

Her annoying roommate finally walked through the door, the Ivory Board in hand. Her other arm was still wrapped in a bright pink cast that was covered in graffiti. I smirked, knowing she had not touched Buffy since I broke it and had been more respectful of their shared space.

She nonchalantly plopped the board on the bed and jotted down a note on top. Then she grabbed a duffle bag with the word "PINK" on it, slung it over her uninjured arm, and ran out of the room. A simple color name written so enthusiastically on a bag; I furrowed my brows at the strange fashion in the human world. Buffy would not have to worry about clothes much longer. I pushed the confusion away and read the note.

Buff,
She gave it back gladly. It's yours.
Keep it away from me. You owe me, whore.

> *Happy Hoe-lloween. Say hi to your mom and your slutty little demon boyfriend.*
> *-Neveah*

I smiled, knowing my little dream had not tried to run away after all. I would still punish her for not telling me where she was going. *Then again...* I sniffed her pillow. *Fuck, I'm going soft.*

I found the pipe and bag of herbs she always puffed on, grabbing the few seeds embedded in the bunch. I would make her a garden and craft her a more deserving pipe, an elegant one fit for the Queen of Dreams. I squeezed the seeds in my hand, and it disappeared for safekeeping.

The blue box on Buffy's desk came to life with a touch, making the glass glow, and I left her a message in her *email*. Smiling, I returned to the Dream World.

The beach shook as my feet fell into the sand in front of the main cavern. As soon as I entered, it was apparent that Overton was back on duty and took a proper knee to greet me.

"Your Grace. I apologize for my outburst. Of course, you have your reasons. It was not my place to question you."

My eyebrows shot up in surprise. "Thank you. What is the update on the hunt for the Sandman?"

"No sign of him."

"Have they tried the south island? The one with the dusty mountains?"

"There is a squad heading that way. It is a few days out."

I flipped the red crystal gauges in my fingers over and over again. "Anything else?"

"No."

"You are excused. I will turn in for the night."

Overton knelt, painfully digging his knee into the cavern floor before he rose slowly, legs trembling. I turned, shaking my head and smiling. *Slater really did a number on him.*

I walked through the doors of our new room, admiring the work I had done for my little dream. I knew exactly where I would bend Buffy over first, where I would tie her little wrists, and where she would take my seed when her body was ready for my spawn. My cocks ached for her, but rest called for me. My third sleep was late by hours.

I laid my head down and fell into a deep sleep. Her screams of agony haunted my dreams. The pain was worse than I imagined. She was bleeding through her clothes and crying, alone in her car. It went on for what felt like an eternity. I woke up with a startle, the sun setting over the human world again.

She was suffering. No wonder she wanted the board. She needed me. I climbed from my bed and charged out of the room, searching for Khadijah or *anyone* to help me locate her.

I barged into the blackness of the temple below the floors. Their humming and chanting stopped, incense curling through the air. The eyeless faces of countless dream healers turned toward me as I walked through the aisle of kneeling students and their superiors. Khadijah was sitting on a plush red pillow at the far side of the room.

"Take a seat," she offered.

I did, resting myself on a blue pillow across from her. "She is not well. She is not home, and I need to get to her."

"Has she summoned you?"

"Would I be here if she had?"

"You can do nothing without her using a spell or a high board to summon you specifically. I have given you every means to access her, Your Grace."

"You can see her dreams. You can dream walk. Tell me what she is dreaming of. Speak to her in her sleep. Tell her to cast the spell again."

"My King, she has not slept yet tonight," she stated matter-of-factly. It was late in her world. *Why wouldn't she be asleep by now?* She loved sleep. The transition would have made her even more eager to go to bed. Something was wrong.

"*Make* her sleep," I insisted angrily.

"That is a sleep demon's power, not a dream healer's. We heal the sleeping and protect their dreams. That is all."

"I need to know where she is. I need to see her. She is *mine!*"

"It is the night of their Halloween. Perhaps she is out with old friends as humans do around this time. Either way, it is *our* Samhain; we need not be distracted. I urge you to focus on your kingdom tonight. If the girl is as strong as you say, she will transition fine. As soon as she falls asleep, I will ensure she has wonderful dreams and that her body heals from the day's breaking."

I stood and made my way to the door. I stopped short, inhaling a tendril of incense smoke from a student's small pyre. I pictured her in my head, blew the smoke out, and held the image in my palm. Tears covered her face in a mask of agony. I kept it close as I rose from the tunnels to the beach, where sleep demons covered the sand.

Everyone was haunting via the Sacred Sands or summoned by spell or board tonight. My power was full. I had no need for a haunt, and on Samhain, I stayed to rule and oversee the festivities. I sat on a high dune, watching my people do their best work.

The night went well—perhaps too well. There was not a sign of the Sandman. There were no mishaps. No attempts to steal the Sacred Sands or overthrow our kingdom. The filches were cooperative and thorough. No new filches were made either; each demon took only what they needed from the humans and gave back to them in kind—giving and receiving equally.

The entire night, I watched. Meteorites flashed through the sky with long, fiery tails that sparkled. Some crashed against the crystal moon, sending diamond-like dust raining down to the ocean. The water churned it slowly toward our shore, and it became part of our beach. I smiled at the beautiful sight and couldn't wait to share it with Buffy.

I turned to go back inside, the holiday long over. But as I stepped through the threshold, my gauges hummed in her sweet voice. She called for me weakly. I ran onto the shore and looked to the moon. Closing my eyes, I let the power of the Ivory Board take me to her.

Her room took shape.

13

BUFFY

When I got back to the dorm room, it was dark. Only a few students remained on campus; after all, Halloween Break had started a few days prior. But I couldn't sleep in my childhood room another night.

I rushed out in the morning, telling my mother I had extra credit due to make up for the heart diagram I never turned in. While that was true, the reality was that I didn't want the Sandman to touch me ever again. The thought of his dead fingers crawling inside me gave me a sour taste along my gums that promised vomit.

I needed Bane. I wanted to sink into his shimmering white sand and never leave his side. I needed him more than ever. I walked through the threshold, worried that when I did see him, he wouldn't want me after the Sandman tainted me. *No, Bane's more devoted to me than that.*

My computer screen was dark. I walked over to it, tapping the mouse to wake the monitor. I sat in my chair with tears welling in my eyes, slightly short of breath, and my throat scratchy. When I opened my email, my heart skipped a beat. There was a new message from an unknown sender. I clicked on it.

> READ IT OUT LOUD:
> 'RISE, RISE, DEMON OF SLEEP.
> THE MOON KING COMES TO TAKE HIS QUEEN.
> SPIRIT TO BONE, GHOST TO FLESH.
> HE CLAIMS HIS BRIDE.
> NEVER WAKE AGAIN.'
>
> OPEN THE BOX AND GET TO BED.
> SLEEP NAKED AND CALL FOR ME.
> DO THIS OR NEVER SLEEP AGAIN.

I huffed out a laugh and wiped tears from my cheek. Again with his threats, as if I wasn't pathetically obsessed with him—as if I wasn't terrified of him abandoning me when he heard I bought a cheap board and let some demonic creep make me cum.

The only question was: what box? I looked around the dark room. My eyes landed on a wooden box with a note on my bed. It had Bane's board in it, and the note was from Neveah.

I threw it open, pulling the board and mouse out. I left them near my pillow, undressed, and climbed into bed. I lay on a tilt, wincing at the pressure against my sore spine and open wounds. Wiping more tears away from my eyes, I remained still with the mouse clutched to my chest. I took a deep breath and made sure I was collected, promising myself I wouldn't let this gorgeous demon see me ugly cry. Finally, I worked up the nerve.

"Bane," I whispered.

The bed groaned, and the room grew frigid. His shadow appeared first, and then his body took form. From spirit to bone, from ghost to flesh, he was over me on hands and knees, smirking. He cupped my chin, pressing his fingers into the back of my head.

"There's my little dream," he said before releasing that T-rex growl he always did.

Instantly, I choked. My face soured. I threw my arms around him and cried hysterically. Fighting to get a full breath of air with each gasp, I hyperventilated. My body shook as I clung to him, and he lifted me into his lap.

So much for staying calm. What can I say? I was overwhelmed by what happened the night prior, and I finally felt safe for whatever reason.

He threw his arms around me tight, hitting the wounded flesh the Sandman had sliced open over my spikes. I cried out in pain, arching my back and burying my face in his neck. He eased his hold, looking over my shoulder to see the raw, tender skin stretching around them.

"You cut your spikes out? They would have pushed through the skin on their own. It would have hurt less, my little dream. Not everything can be rushed so easily," he said, stroking my hair and kissing my temple. "Let your body change for you."

I shook my head, still nuzzled against him and too ashamed to look him in the face. "I didn't..." After a moment of trying to get any other words to form, I let out a horrific sob and dug my fingertips into his back, falling deeper into his arms. His cold skin against my face calmed me. But he grabbed my shoulders and pulled me away gently, cocking his head and studying my expression.

"What happened?" Bane questioned with furrowed brows. He looked fit to kill someone. Tears tunneled down the blush on my cheeks as I caught my breath to speak. I gazed at his chest and tried to form words.

"You left me alone. I needed you. I needed to see you, and you weren't there!"

"I had to prepare for your arrival. I have obligations back home, and I would not have been able to keep my hands off—."

"*No*... you don't understand. I needed you, and Neveah gave away the board. I had to force her to get it back, but I couldn't wait, so I..." My breath galloped for a moment, and I covered my face.

He pulled my hands down and raised my chin. His expression was like stone. "You *what*?"

Finally, I looked into his eyes. I wanted to give him at least that much. "I bought a cheap Ouija board from the mall and called for you, but..."

He swallowed hard and shook his head just an inch. "No..."

"The demon that came wasn't you, and he... He dragged me under. He..." I couldn't say anymore. Memories of what the Sandman did flooded my memory. It was like I was there again, reliving every humiliating moment.

"Who? Who is he? What did he do to you?" Bane demanded. His blue and black eyes simmered with rage.

Just then, I burst into a coughing fit. It was like hacking up shards of glass. Burnt-orange sand spurted from my mouth, getting caught in my throat on the way up, and I gagged.

His eyes were wide as he held out his hand and let it run through his fingers. He squeezed his hand shut, making the sand disappear.

I gasped for air. My lungs noticeably lost some capacity. "He said he's going to do it again. And he's going to kill me!"

"Do *what* again?" he growled.

"He..." I choked on the words. I couldn't say them. I cowered, covering my face and chest and rocking in his lap as I let out a hideous cry.

"Shhh. Be calm. You don't have to say it. I will see your memory," he said, placing his massive hands over my ears and pulling my forehead to his. My heart raced. I knew he would see it. He would see that I came on the Sandman's fingers and swallowed his cum.

"No!" I begged with a hoarse voice.

But he had already entered my mind—the part of the subconscious that stores memories to become dreams.

Bane was there in the moment. I could see him as if he was standing over the events, observing every second of it. He saw my stupid lingerie and how I hurried to get ready for him. His brow sprung up in pleasant surprise. Then his face turned gaunt as he saw me getting wrestled out of my robe and dragged under the bed. He saw the Sandman touch me, slice me, brand me, take me, and condemn me. My demon flinched every time I screamed for him. His eyes were wide, but he never looked away. Not once. He heard the Sandman's lethal demands, his voice distorted in the vision.

"Tell Bane that the Sandman wants what is his, or I will take what is most precious to him."

He shook, lips twitching as he saw me wake with the slap and sob uncontrollably, bleeding from my face, back, and center. He saw me wail in pain as I tried to peel the dried blood on my robe off my raw back. And he watched me burn the clothes outside, curl up on the shower floor, and cry quietly so I didn't wake my mother.

Withdrawing from my mind, he pulled away, anger etched into his face. I shook my head, humiliated.

"Bane... I'm—"

He grabbed the nape of my neck tight, pulling it back. "Sleep!" he yelled.

There was no fighting *this* command. My body went limp, and in no time, I was falling through the dark sky of the Dream World. But I was in Bane's arms as his feet slammed into the diamond dust beach. A plume of shimmering sand kicked twenty feet above us like a mushroom cloud sparkling in the light of the crystal moon.

He had dressed me in a white, cashmere halter dress that dipped between my breasts. It hung loose, flowing in the wind. Bane held me to his chest as he charged away from the turbulent, indigo water and toward the vine-covered dunes. I didn't know where he was taking me or what he was going to do. The only thing I was certain of was that Bane was livid, and I panicked.

"Bane, I'm sorry. I didn't—"

"Do not ever apologize for that again," he demanded flatly. "Just rest. I have you now. Everything is going to be okay."

My eyes shut with relief, and I cried. I laid my face against his cool chest, tears the only thing between us. The moonlight inched away as we descended into a tunnel of charcoal stone. Torches with blue flames and crackling yellow embers lined the cavernous walls. I heard commotion ahead, and it grew louder the deeper he walked.

Finally, we entered a large common space with a glass ceiling that allowed the crystal moon to shower light on every surface. The commotion stopped, but someone approached us.

"She is not marked! She cannot be here, Your Grace. It is a sacred place."

"Enough! Bring me the healers!" Bane's words echoed, vibrating through my entire body. "*Now!*"

The person fumbled over their words. "Of course. My apologies. Wh-which healers?"

"*All* of them!"

Bane carried me past a curved wall and up a short stack of stairs. Finally, he swung open large ivory doors, charging through. Somehow, we were far above the beach in a dome-shaped room with clear crystal walls. A plush bed lay in the center. It was the most gorgeous bed I had ever seen, with a massive ivory canopy from which purple morning glories hung.

The softest fabric I could dream of, filled with feather-like petals, covered the mattress, and a silver plate with purple oil was placed on top of it. Podiums were erected along the rounded walls and lit by large blue flames, crackling with yellow embers, illuminating the beautiful space.

Bane set me down gently on the bed. "Where are they?" he yelled, moving the silver plate to a side table.

The room was suddenly filled with eyeless figures; their slick silver-blue skin stretched over empty sockets. They stood with perfect posture, and their hands were tucked into the large sleeves of their white robes. As a collective, they bowed to Bane, and one hurried to his side. The healer was tall and thin with black lips and hollow cheeks.

"My King, we came as soon as possible." They straightened their back and slowly turned toward me. Chills ran through my gut at the eyeless face that seemed to stare into my soul. "Unmarked, Your Grace?"

"The Sandman cursed her last night when I came to *you* for help. *Fix* it."

The healer bowed, glided over to me, and rested a hand on my head. They saw everything. I relived it again with yet another audience. But the healer didn't flinch. They only bowed their head in pity.

I sat in shame as their long, slick fingers slid from my temple, and a tear fell from my cheek. With a nod, all the healers glided over. I backed away, terrified of the strange beings. Bane climbed on the bed, sat with his legs crossed, and pulled me onto his lap with my back to the others. My legs and arms wrapped around him, and the healers studied my wounds.

"He sliced the spikes out of her skin. Heal her pain first." One healer removed a bowl filled with a salve from their sleeve; it seemed to come out of thin air. They pasted the ointment over each spike, and despite my best efforts, I winced as they touched me.

Bane looked me in the eye, nose-to-nose. "Khadijah is our master healer. She can help you. You are safe now," he reassured me in a grave tone, brushing hair away from my face. I winced again as a healer cleansed a spike and another pasted salve over it. "You are doing so good, my little dream. You can do this. I have given you worse."

I nodded, resting my forehead on his.

"I am afraid that is *not* the worst of it," Khadijah remarked as she ran her hand over my lower back, the same place I felt a thousand bee stings when the Sandman pressed on it. "He has imprinted a curse contract on her skin."

The morning after being dragged under the bed, I saw the Stüssy S and tribal art stamped across my lower back. I thought it was his way of mentally torturing me, leaving me with a tramp stamp bearing an S to remind me of him—the *Sandman*. It seems that wasn't the case.

Khadijah traced her fingers over the tattoo as if reading Braille. I coughed, sand spurting from my mouth again. I gagged and choked as another healer floated it away from my face. Bane stopped it, gripped it tight, and made it disappear. When I finished hacking, someone offered me water. I sipped it and gasped. They placed their hands on my sides and pressed firmly.

"She is filling with sand," they said to Khadijah.

Khadijah finished tracing her fingers along the tattoo and nodded. "And so she will."

"What do you mean '*so she will?*'" Bane growled.

"The contract reads that you must return the Sacred Sands to the Sandman by three moons, or she will die. Her lungs will slowly fill. Buffy cannot die before that, even if she tries. She will die slowly and suffer. Only when the Sandman has every grain of Sacred Sand in his possession will she be free of this fate and live. Tonight was the first of three."

It felt as though all the air was sucked out of me, like a punch to the gut. "Wh-what are the Sacred Sands? Wha—?"

"They give me reign over the Dream World. There is one grain from every shore, mountain, ocean depth, and desert on earth. It is the very tool that grants sleep demons and spirits access to your world without being summoned by a board or spell. It was split once between several lords. The Sandman kept the most. But he became hungry for more power. Instead of helping children fall asleep, he sent a monster to kill young humans in their dreams with long knife-like fingers. Feasting on their flesh made him strong in your world. We could not stand for it. It had to stop."

"Stop killing humans? Why would you care about humans? Sleep demons just come to terrorize us."

Bane smiled in a way that made my heart leap. He leaned forward, grabbing my neck and pulling me in close. "Terrorizing humans keeps us fertile and strong. That's how we reproduce and make seed for your womb. And it is fate for many sleep demons that we will eventually find our perfect partners. We dream only of their faces our whole lives, so when we finally see them, we know. And then, we are ravenous for their body. If our dream is a human, they start to change once they offer themselves to us," he explained, stroking my spikes.

They didn't hurt anymore. They actually felt amazing, and my core ran hot for him as I breathed heavily.

His face turned serious again, and he pulled away. "*And* when our dream is human, we mark them to join us here, and they become immortal demons of the Dream World. Killing the humans was a threat to our very existence and yours. We have always been a peaceful people, but he was waging war. I led an army against him and confiscated his Sacred Sands.

He lost all power to rule or move into your world without passage from humans. It's fitting that he did so with a cheap cut of cardboard. But he slipped away before I could capture and bind him to our world.

"Any lord that was left bowed to me as King of the Dream World. They gave me their Sacred Sand so that I could monitor who enters and exits your world and why. That way, we could be sure no one allied with the Sandman and gave him passage. The Sacred Sands are protected here better than anywhere else. Now he wants them back. All of it."

I looked at Bane and realized there was too much at stake. At that moment, I was preparing to die for him and the people he was sworn to protect.

"Your Grace, she needs to be bathed to prevent infection," Khadijah advised.

"Fill it hot. She likes her skin to turn red," Bane replied without taking his eyes off me.

It took only a wave of a hand to fill the steaming bath that lay against the crystal wall behind the bed. The healers left the room, and finally, we were alone.

Bane scooped me up, his hands cupping my ass, to carry me to the bath full of fragrant herbs and petals.

"You can't give him what he wants," I urged him.

"Oh, I will give him *exactly* what he wants."

14

BANE

I stepped into the bath and lowered Buffy onto my lap, positioning her legs to rest on either side of my hips and taking care to keep her raw spikes as dry as possible. Her dress dissolved in the water as she settled in, and I removed the last piece of fabric from behind her neck and dropped it in to disappear.

She looked calmer, with her eyes closed and her lips barely parted. Her emotions were a void. That was okay for the moment. As long as I could keep her from misery, I was satisfied with her comfort for the night. It would take a lot to heal her heart, but I had the skeleton of my plan created. The Sandman was going to fucking pay for this. I shoved my anger away, focusing on her.

I took a soft cloth from the side of the bath and soaked it in the soap bin. Then I moved it up her chest slowly, making hot bubbles slide down her breasts. I cupped steaming water in my cold palm and rubbed it down her front. When I finished, I pulled her gently against my chest.

"Come here," I murmured softly. She did, resting her cheek on my shoulder and looking out of the crystal wall. I squeezed water over her head, letting it roll down her neck until her hair was soaked. I lathered the wash serum into her roots with my claws. I tugged on her hair lightly, and the tension released the stress in her scalp. She moaned, feeling relaxed.

"How did we get so high?" Her lips moved against my shoulder with each word.

I released the tension, moved my hand, and tugged again in a different spot. "We are in the crystal moon, my love. This is one of the many bumps on its surface."

"The moon? How?" she asked softly, furrowing her brows. She looked at the distant, bubbling, and turbulent sea. The moonlight made everything below sparkle.

"I told you I had to get everything ready for your arrival. I had my best mage help me build a portal in my doorway leading here. Then I carved out a pocket on the moon's surface and built this room from it. Now the moon is yours, my little dream."

I kissed her head as I rinsed the bubbles from her hair with the cloth, the serum leaving the strands soft. My fingers combed through the locks easily. "Do you like it?"

Buffy laughed, nuzzling my shoulder as she answered weakly with a sniffle, "You're asking if I like living in a crystal moon? It's the most beautiful thing I've ever seen, Bane. I love it."

"The bedding is filled with feathered dandelions. You will never sleep on anything more comfortable. I had the filches harvest them, and I stuffed it myself," I divulged, rubbing the cloth down her sides and carefully washing her back. The salve had soaked into her skin and numbed the raw spikes enough, but I needed to clean them more.

"Thank you. You didn't have—"

"Shhh. It gives me joy to do this."

"Bane," she said, lifting her head from my shoulder. Her sclerae were nearly black, and her irises were blue with rounded slits for pupils. I smiled. She was almost done changing; I knew she could take it. She was beautiful, with silver-blue skin, tiny, pointed ears with delicate gauges, adorable, studded spikes in her lips, and a plump forked tongue that I couldn't wait to feel against mine. She took my breath away, and I had to fight to inhale.

"Yes, my little dream?" I whispered, cupping her cheek. My large fingers extended past her pointed ear, and she kissed the heel of my palm.

She reached between her legs, pulling her lips apart, and lifted her hips. She rubbed her center over my first cock, kissing me softly. It twitched awake, and my second cock perked up and coiled in excitement. I dug my fingers into her sides.

"Fuck me before I die, or everything I've gone through will have been for nothing. I don't want him to be the last person inside me. I just want to feel you before... it happens," she continued weakly, a tear rolling down her lip. She sniffled and leaned in to kiss me again. "Mark me as yours. That's how I want to go."

I hissed and smiled, adjusting my position in excitement and reaching down to tame my eager, spirited cock with a firm squeeze. I let out a long breath through my nose.

"Calm down," I sternly admonished the spirit as it whirled in my grip. It obeyed. My gaze slowly trailed up her wet body. She was the most beautiful thing I had ever laid my eyes on. I met her gaze and cupped her cheeks, staring into her soul. I would take no pleasure from Buffy's body until I avenged her.

"You are not going to die. But if I mark you before I finish dealing with that fuck, it will be when your lungs are nearly full, and you are panicking, failing to catch your breath as you inch closer to death." My cock twitched, but she looked confused. "Not tonight. You have been through too much. It is time to rest and heal. Let me take care of you." I washed her legs next.

Her face morphed further into bafflement as the soft cloth glided over her skin. "Why do you love to see me suffer?"

"I have never enjoyed watching you suffer," I said with offense.

"You've always loved to see me terrified. Why? Why don't you want me safe if you care so much?"

I sat up, tugging her hips to me. The water sloshed around us. "'*Terror*' and '*unsafe*' are two very different things," I said sternly

"They're both terrible to feel."

"No. The world conditioned you to think terror is bad. But terror fills your body with endorphins, adrenaline, and dopamine; it heightens your senses and makes you *feel*," I said, rubbing my thumbs up her inner thighs. I worked the cloth along her injured center, cleaning her gently. She tensed, breathing with nervous excitement.

"*Unsafe* means you are at risk of serious harm or death. *Suffering* means you experienced only misery and no willful pleasure. *Neither* is the case." I paused, making sure I had her full attention as I rubbed the cloth in circles over her clit. "I have filled you with much terror, but you have *always* been safe with me. And once I take my revenge on him, you will be untouchable." I leaned in close to whisper, "*But never to me.*" Moving the cloth to her tight ass, I pressed in hard, and she let out a soft moan. "You will *never* escape my touch."

She looked at me, eyes burning with lust. I pulled my hands away from between her legs, and she exhaled heavily. I picked her up, letting the water drip down and allowing us to dry quickly. Her arms were snug around my neck, her legs wrapped around my waist.

"Do you trust me?" I asked. She leaned in and kissed me deeply. The feeling of her forked tongue sliding across mine nearly made my knees buckle. They twisted against each other, and I groaned as the sensitive space between my tongue tips tingled with pleasure.

"Yes," she purred, breaking our connection only long enough to answer me. She kissed me faster, sucking in my bottom lip. She rocked her hips, grinding her center against my hard lengths. I carried her to the bed, gently pulling back the covers and laying her down. She winced as the pressure hit her back, and I tilted her. She nuzzled into the blanket.

"It's time to rest, my little dream," I insisted, pulling her arms and legs from me. Buffy looked ready to cry. "I'm right here," I reassured, crawling in the bed next to her. I grabbed the bowl of salve and reapplied it over her spikes. She didn't flinch once as her face pressed into my chest.

Then I grabbed the oil, rubbing it along her shoulder. I had spent the prior three days extracting every drop of oil from the flower petals and making it for her.

She turned her head, enjoying the fragrance and humming. "That's beautiful. What is it?"

"Just a little gift." I smiled proudly as I stroked it over her collarbone. "I was going to give it to you as a marking gift, but I want you to have it now." My hand found its way to the front of her neck, and I massaged the oil in as I wrapped my hand around her throat, squeezing tight. "Do you feel *safe?*"

She looked up at me, submission obvious in her eyes, and nodded. I kissed her, slowly squeezing her throat closed before releasing my hold. I laid on my back and pulled her close.

She winced a few times as her sharp cramps came and went. They seemed better, but I still put silver water to her lips, and she sipped it, sighing in comfort. Each time she would cough up sand, I'd make it disappear for safekeeping.

To calm her, I told her about the moon and how it picked up light from stars far away, reflecting it on our land. I told her how the meteors that crashed into the moon break off tiny shards of crystal that fall to the ocean and get ground in the tempestuous water until they become our sand.

"This is a low-hanging moon, almost fully in our atmosphere. It's close enough to make the water turbulent but high enough to make the air too thin up here. You will be immortal soon, so if the crystal breaks, you will be okay. It will not break, though. I shielded—"

I looked down to see her sleeping. Willingly falling asleep next to a demon like me was the ultimate display of trust and affection. My heart skipped a beat. Honor filled me. Typically seeing Buffy sleep would make me hungry to fuck her. But I would not cum again until I avenged her. That night, I took comfort in knowing she was safe. She was comfortable. She was *mine*.

I lay awake, planning vengeance against the Sandman. I was close to figuring out exactly how I could protect my dream forever from someone who could not die.

15

BUFFY

I woke up on my bed, lying on my side. I opened my eyes, disappointed that I wasn't in the crystal moon beside Bane. I closed my eyes again, remembering him, and rolled over, pressing the spikes into the bed. I smirked and let out a groan. They didn't hurt nearly as bad. In fact, they stimulated every nerve in my body—*every* nerve. I rubbed my back deeper into the mattress, and my breathing picked up.

"I didn't give you permission to do that, now did I?" a deep voice asked. My eyes shot wide open to see Bane sitting at the head of my bed, leaning into the dark corner. "It may feel nice, but if you tear the skin open and it gets infected before you are marked, we will have a problem."

"You're here... when the sun is nearly up," I observed, standing on my bed to close the makeshift curtains tighter. His eyes devoured my naked body. I blushed, walking toward him. He rested his hands on my hips as he looked up at me. I was safe with him and knew he'd never let the Sandman touch me again.

"I can not stay. I will send you instructions later. For now, I need to assign you a protector that lives in this world. You are not to leave his side."

"A protector? Who?"

"The gay one you are always with will do. I sent him an *eye-mail* from your blue box. He will be here soon."

"You sent... *Blue box?* You mean my *computer?* Wait, what *gay* guy?"

"The blonde one with the very white teeth."

"*Harvey?* Harvey isn't gay—*is* he?" That made so much sense. I ran my fingers through my hair, adding it all up. There was a knock at my door.

"That is him. Do not give him warning," Bane instructed and disappeared.

I looked around, wondering what the hell I was supposed to tell my friend. I threw on an oversized Slipknot t-shirt and a black lace thong before running to open the door.

"Hey—*Holy* hell, Buffy! What happened to you?" he shouted, looking at my blue-tinted skin and altered eyes.

I grabbed his arm and tugged him inside, closing the door behind him. He dropped his skateboard. It landed upside down, revealing a bottom covered in anarchy and green alien stickers and graffiti. Harvey swallowed hard as he stared.

"If I told you I'm destined to couple with a sleep paralysis demon and currently going through an awkward demon growth phase, would you believe me?" I queried, pulling my long black hair into a messy bun.

"I'm sorry, what?"

"Here, sit with me." I sat down and patted the bed. He followed with a slack jaw and kept his distance. "Umm, okay. So, here's the scoop. I'm in some trouble. There's a bad person—*thing* trying to kill me, and I need someone to watch my back until we have a plan ready. And Bane picked you, so—"

"Someone's trying to kill you, and you emailed me instead of calling the cops?"

"There's nothing they can do, trust me."

"And... and what am I supposed to do, *charm* them to death?" Harvey asked sarcastically, throwing his hands up and looking at me sideways.

"Or maul them," Bane interjected.

Harvey spun around, startled to find a massive demon towering over him. "Sh-sh-shit!" he stuttered.

Bane's palm made contact with his chest, pushing him onto the bed. Harvey froze, unable to move, as he looked up at the naked demon in horror. I could almost feel the fear coming off of him.

"This will hurt," Bane warned before slowly bending down and baring his sharp canines. He took his time biting into Harvey's flesh.

I drew in a sharp breath and tried to pull him off. "Bane, what are you doing? Stop!"

Bane did not stop but grabbed my wrist and squeezed it tight. My friend writhed under him in anguish, and I tried to turn away, but the demon held my wrist too hard. After a long while, Bane removed his fangs from Harvey's shoulder, blood dripping from his mouth. He hovered over Harvey for a long moment, soaking up the terror and pain in his eyes. Then he stood, smiling down at him, his cock growing hard as both Harvey and I trembled in an orgy of fear.

Harvey groaned and panted in pain, still immobile. Veins popped from his skin. His hair thickened, and his nails sharpened.

"I do not have long, so listen closely, boy," Bane began. Harvey's insides shifted under his skin, and he groaned again. "As King of the Dream World, a guardian of the moon spirits, I can produce alpha werewolves. You can shift whenever you need to. It does not take effort. If the Sandman comes near her, you bite his fucking dick off first and then keep him incapacitated while Buffy calls for me. He is immortal. You can not kill him, so do not try to go for his neck. Understand?"

Harvey just looked up at him in horror.

"I said, 'do you understand?'" Bane yelled, releasing Harvey from his frozen state.

"Yes..." Harvey muttered with wide eyes, sitting up and backing away. "Wha-what are you?"

"This is Bane... He's my boyfriend, kind of..." I said with guilt lacing my voice. I gave Harvey a sorry look as I glanced between him and his bitten shoulder.

Bane stalked over to me slowly, looking at me like I had just stepped out of line. I backed away, bumping into my desk. My mouse fell off and dangled by its wire, the ball inside spinning erratically. *I'm safe with him,* I reminded myself as fear rose inside me. He grabbed my neck and lifted me from the ground. My throat was constricted tight in his grasp. I struggled to breathe as my face flushed, clawing at his forearm.

"I am no *boy*. I am your *owner*. Do not forget that," he growled. Then he kissed me. At first, it was tender and soft despite my legs kicking in panic. But he slid his long, forked tongue down my throat. He flicked it over my uvula repeatedly, making me retch hard in response. He rubbed his free hand over my panties and kept his lips firmly against mine as I struggled to breathe, holding back my instinct to vomit as he triggered my gag reflex over and over again. He carried out this punishment for a long, uncomfortable moment. Knowing I couldn't die before the third night, he reveled in my terror as I squirmed and choked. My body ran hot for him. *I am safe with him.*

Finally, he pulled his lips away, a string of spit hanging between us. He smiled up at my pink-tinted face; my feet twitched as they dangled in the air. I couldn't decide what was more beautiful, the way he tortured me so sweetly or those lips when he smiled at how well I took it. He kept rubbing my panties. My vision tunneled, and my eyes started to tingle from the pressure.

"I am sorry I have to leave, my love. Wait by the computer for instructions. If you need me, *recite the spell* this time."

Then he threw me onto my bed. By the time I landed, Bane was gone. I gasped, hungry for air and clutching my neck. Between gasps, I could only cough up small heaps of sand. Bane had enchanted it to disappear, so I didn't have to see it. My face was crimson, and tears collected as I tried to rid my throat of the burning feeling.

Harvey clambered to my side, patting my back and urging me to take slow, deep breaths. Gradually, I calmed down, and I slowly wheezed. If I was honest with myself, it was a rush, and my thighs heated. I wiped my nose on my sleeve and looked up at my friend. His shoulder bled a shimmering crimson.

"What the fuck was that, Buffy?"

"It's a long story."

He just looked at me, wondering where the hell we had to be at 7:00 AM on Halloween Break.

I offered a tired smile and huffed. "Well, it started with Neveah bringing home this ivory board."

I told him the whole story. Having someone I could confide in about all of it was cathartic. Harvey, however, was horrified to hear what Bane had put me through, insisting he was sick and abusive. He wasn't wrong. The demon loved to scare me, torture me, and control me. But I was addicted to it and addicted to Bane. There was a sense of worship in the way he took his time terrorizing me until I came for him. Nothing had ever turned me on more. I loved it, and I knew he cared.

"I... think I'm falling in love with him, Harv, and—" I broke off into a coughing fit. Piles of sand poured out of my mouth. He patted my back and held me close. "I'm sorry I dragged you into this."

"I'm not. I'm glad I can be here for you. You're going to be okay, Buff. I won't let anyone get to you."

"Bold coming from someone who hasn't even shifted yet," I quipped, spitting sand-laced saliva into my trash can and panting as my lung capacity lessened by the minute.

He furrowed his brows and sighed. "Yeah, I'm still wrapping my head around that."

"You should try. Better get a hang of it now before we run into the Sandman."

Harvey scrubbed his face, took a deep breath, and stood up. Wasting no time, he rolled up his sleeves and closed his eyes. Within seconds, he shifted from wolf to human again before his shredded clothes had time to reach the floor. His face was in shock from the undoubtedly strange feeling.

My mouth hung open in disbelief.

"That was... weird. But he's right. That's not hard at all."

"You... you have a knot in your dick now." I pointed to his exposed member with a nod. "Unless you've always..."

Harvey covered himself indignantly. I jumped off the bed, dug through a basket of folded laundry, and threw him a pair of sweats. He hurried to clothe himself. After an awkward silence, we laughed, picked up his shredded clothes, and threw them in the wastebasket, which was clear of the orange sand.

He saw me walking around in a black lace thong and a shirt. I had seen him in his whole birthday suit, dick and all. We trauma-bonded all morning. Yet here we were with zero chemistry. If he *was* gay, why wouldn't he tell me?

"So, what now?" Harvey stared at his hands as he shifted them back and forth from claw-bearing paws to regular football player hands. He furrowed his brows in wonder.

"We wait."

"Does that involve food? Because I feel like tearing a live deer to shreds."

My eyes went wide. "We can't leave. Bane told me to wait here, and I can't leave your side," I stated cautiously. "Also, the sun will burn my eyes, so we can't leave before the sun goes down anyway."

"Why are you looking at me like that?"

"I'm just wondering how long until you go full wolf and eat *me*."

"Ew. I have *no* interest in eating *you*. I'm just very hungry for meat, Buffy."

Heavy emphasis on 'you.'

"Is... *my* kind of meat not the type you enjoy?"

Harvey looked at me blankly, then shook his head slightly. "I don't know, Buff. I've been a werewolf for half a day."

"That's not really what I meant."

"Let's just order a pizza, okay?" he said awkwardly, walking over to my clear phone and dialing the shop down the road. I pressed my thumb on the switch hook, disconnecting the call. Pursing his lips, Harvey threw back his head and rolled his neck.

"Harvey, you don't have to tell me, but I just want you to know that if you are... not into that kind of meat, I'm cool with it. Like, *girl* meat, I mean. That's totally fine."

"You think I'm some kind of fag?"

"Harv, if you were, there's nothing wrong with it. I love you. I like girls and guys. I'm not the one to judge you, trust me. I get it."

"No, you don't get it! It's different for girls. If you do it, people think it's hot. You don't get what that's like for a guy, much less a football player. It's not—"

"Hey, hey, hey. Slow your roll. I'm not going to tell anyone. I just... I hope you know you can trust me. And if you can't... I'll probably be dead by tomorrow night anyway, so I'll take it to my grave."

Eyes watering, Harvey let out a laugh, and I threw my arms around him. He hugged me back, kissing the top of my head. "How much do you trust this demon of yours?"

"With my life," I responded, letting go. I turned to the phone and dialed the pizza place. "Meat lovers, extra meat?"

"Yeah," he said, sitting on the edge of my bed, holding his head in his hands and releasing a heavy sigh. "What a fucking day."

We ate and made paper fortune tellers with perverted answers written inside. And, even though I gleefully had no intention of graduating, we did extra credit assignments and studied for finals. A weight had lifted. Aside from my inability to take a complete breath and my constant hacking fits, we had fun. Eventually, night fell. When my email chimed, our mood shifted to something somber.

Harvey opened the email from an unknown sender.

"They have a plan. We better move."

16

BANE

I started my day roughly. And not only because I refused to sleep while Buffy stayed in our bed for the first time, healing from the attack. I didn't want to leave her in her dorm, but I had to deal with the Sandman. At least I had complete faith in her wolf protector, *Harvey.*

Early in the morning, I held her in my arms, dreading the moment I had to take her back. Before she had to wake and leave for her world, Overton knocked quietly and entered the room. I hushed him, rested my hand on her head, and kept her asleep. Then I beckoned him closer.

"You are growing too weak, Your Grace. She must return. I am so sorry," he whispered.

"Five more minutes. She is cranky when she wakes before seven."

"Shall I retrieve the prisoner so you can refuel?"

"Not yet. I am stronger than I look, Overton. And I have not even fucked her." I glanced down and kissed Buffy's head, pulling the plush covers over her chin. She was so fucking sexy when she slept, and I did not want to share that image with anyone. Not even with a receiver like Overton, who preferred to feed off *being* terrorized. "Call the filches in. The search is over."

"And what of their prize?"

"I will discuss it with them when I get back."

"Back? Your Grace, I must impress upon you, leaving for the human world—"

"Is necessary to ensure her safety until I have the Sandman dealt with," I said calmly, raising my brow. "It is almost time for her to wake. Call in the filches. I will be back before they arrive."

He stepped out of the room.

I pulled the comforter down, exposing her naked body from head to toe and running my hand up her thigh. If these were normal circumstances, I would keep her asleep and try to make her body cum for me, unconscious. I bet she sounded amazing while cumming in her sleep.

I ducked my head to her chest, sucking at her nipples. She moaned, and my heart pounded. I burned the image of her resting into my brain to make a smoke mural later. It would be the first of her as an almost wholly transitioned demoness and the first one of her in our bed. I wanted it splayed across my ceiling, enchanted so only I could see it.

I held her close, her tits tightening in my mouth. I fought the urge to fuck her as she stirred, moaning sleepily. I released her nipple and pressed my forehead against her chest. It had to wait. I closed my eyes.

When I opened them, we were in her bed. The sun was rising,

and my eyes burned. I scoffed, backing into a dark corner. From my perch, I managed to send an email to the boy, moving the keys from across the bed.

She was safe; her trusted friend was with her and could take down demons in their world. Not me, though. The new wolf sat in shock as I held Buffy by the neck, knowing very well I would kill him if he stopped me.

Buffy loved it when I terrorized her, getting wet as she struggled in my grip. But much like when I got lost in her body as she slept, I let the last kiss linger a little too long; she was my weakness. I had to leave with haste before I became a filch, so I tossed her down, disappearing before she hit the bed.

I landed in the sand outside of the main cavern, nearly depleted of power by keeping Buffy overnight and leaving with her in the morning. Weaker than I had been in a long while, I headed quickly to the prison hold with feeble knees. I dragged the scrawny dweeb that called himself Skeeter, kicking and screaming, onto the beach.

He begged. He apologized. He cried. All I had to do was stand over him, and his fear fueled me. I panted as my energy slowly returned. I bared my teeth and released a low rumble from my chest to move things along, feeling stronger by the second. The human was an endless pit of cowardness, urinating on himself at the sight of a claw.

Slater approached, but I didn't look up at him. Seeing me clearly in fine health and almost done, he engaged. "How do you keep this human here without spending your energy?"

"I separated his spirit from his body and carved up the latter in the human world. He is as good as dead to the humans but alive and bound to the Dream World forever. He will never take from us again. He will never know rest or peace again."

Skeeter looked as though I was squeezing his heart tight. Despair filled him more than the terror. *Hopelessness.* I could not stand it. I cleared his recent memory. Then I grabbed his hair and pulled like I was ripping it from his scalp and roared. He screamed. The returning terror fueled me faster.

"All for insults and empty threats. I look forward to hearing what you have in store for the Sandman when we find him," he said.

I let go of Skeeter's hair and let him fall to the ground sobbing. Then, I let out a sigh. My energy was full, and my bulb was swollen, but my heart was heavy.

"I heard what happened... How is she?"

A pang of guilt tugged at my heart. "She is strong but wounded. I made her an alpha wolf to protect her until we sort out the details of my plan."

Slater nodded, hiding his surprise at me bestowing such a gift upon a random mortal. But this Harvey was not so random. He was worthy of alpha status. I had a sense for it that Slater would not understand.

"The filches are nearly here. What *is* the plan?"

I rubbed a finger over my top lip. "We will get to that soon enough. Grab that for me, will you?" I asked, pointing at Skeeter and turning to the shoreline.

The sickly gray beasts—a hundred or more—rose from the water, sopping wet and inching out of the deep. They stomped onto the shore in squads, dropped to both knees and waited. When Slater dropped Skeeter onto the sand, the group feasted their eyes on him eagerly.

"The search is off. The Sandman will present himself," I announced. Murmurs hummed louder by the moment as the group grew uneasy. "There is the matter of your reward. Your efforts have been invaluable. You will pass the prisoner to a new filch each week. There will be no repeats until each filch has had their turn. If one of you kills him, I will cut off your limbs and toss you in the boils."

The filches smiled with perverse hunger, their decayed teeth oozing with slime.

I spoke louder over their excited exchanges. "To stay alive, you must keep him on land so he will remain stranded on Dusty Island. You will crawl from the water and feed."

"And who is the first to claim him?" one filch asked in a dreadfully scratchy voice. Skeeter whimpered and whined on the ground, shaking.

I siphoned his fear as I answered, "I asked you all to harvest my queen the petals of feathered dandelions on your hunt. One filch delivered the most. *Ren*. You will take the filch prize first."

A tall, thin filch with two locks of hair left stepped forward. He smiled greedily and grabbed the boy. Skeeter screamed, falling to his hands and begging me for mercy.

"If only you knew how to keep your filthy hands off of my dream the first time she told you to," I mused before turning to Ren. "Get him there safely. You have seven nights. The current owner chooses the next filch."

"To do with *whatever* we want?" Ren questioned.

"Of course. You have all served well, and I am grateful. Keep him alive so your fellow filches do not miss out. That is all I command." I turned away, walking toward the cavern of Sacred Sands.

"No! No!" Skeeter screamed as Ren dragged him into the water.

Ren hummed in delight as his strength grew, and the water splashed with the bodies of a hundred filches, all ensuring the boy got to the island safely. The screams gurgled to a halt as Ren dunked him underwater to quiet him. "Quiet!"

"Slater, I need you to trust me," I said as we finally arrived at the Cavern of Sacred Sands. He nodded, looking at the grand sight. The entrance was just as large as the main cavern but sealed with a silver gate and spells. And guards stood at attention around the beach, the Dunes, and far inland to protect the deep tunnels leading to the Sands.

"Of course, I trust you, brother."

"The spells that guard the sands will come down when he is here. That is your first role."

Slater looked at me with wide eyes. "What? Are you mad?"

"And you will prepare the guards to stand down when I give the signal. They must evacuate."

"You would leave the Sacred Sands open for the taking?"

"I intend to give him the sands, Slater. And you will help me."

"He will destroy the human world. He will reduce us all to filches!" Slater urged in hushed tones.

"You think I would allow that to happen, brother?"

"I think love has hindered your judgment."

I laughed. "Perhaps you should listen to the rest of the plan and help me find the faults before jumping to such conclusions."

17

BUFFY

I kept the ivory Ouija board close to my chest and leaned against the door frame of Harvey's Firebird as he drove us back to my hometown. The window was open, and the night air tossed my hair. The wind crashed into my face, making it a little easier to breathe. We had been driving for hours, and my body felt weak. My lips were blue, and it wasn't just from the silver running through my body.

"Stay awake for me, Buffy," Harvey said, talking over the radio. Ironically, Good Riddance by Green Day was playing on two different channels. Catching my frustration, he flipped his sun visor down and fingered through some burned CDs in the holder. "For rock, I have Rammstein or Metallica."

I laughed, remembering the stink Metallica was throwing over Napster, but then I shrugged. He slipped a disc in the CD player; Du Hast blared through the speakers, drawing a smile from me. If he wanted to keep me awake and ready to fight for my life, he made the right choice. I reached out to take his hand, and he squeezed it.

I coughed, the sand catching the wind and hitting me in the face. "Ah!" I shrieked, sitting up and brushing the sand off my eyes and lips before it disappeared under Bane's enchantment. I turned down the volume. "How much longer?"

Harvey looked at the GPS monitor suctioned to the windshield. "Almost there."

He was going as fast as he could, and luckily, the police radar detector, also suctioned to the windshield, hadn't picked up anything but convenience store door alarms.

"This better work..." I grumbled in frustration. Why we had to waste hours to retrieve that piece of shit Ouija board from my mother's house was beyond me. Why the plan had to involve me seeing the Sandman again was *also* beyond me. Maybe I would have been less of a sourpuss if Bane had shared more about what exactly the plan was.

Harvey gave me a sorry look, unsure what to say, and turned back to the road. Gravel crunched under the slowing tires as we turned onto my parents' street. Stopping at the end of the road, he cut off the lights.

"She's home. We'll have to sneak through my window." The engine shut off, and I broke into a coughing fit as soon as I got out.

"You'll wake her up with that cough. I'll go in. Where did you leave it?"

"It's under the bed." I waited by the car. After a long while, Harvey came back out... empty-handed. "What happened?"

"I looked everywhere. It's not there."

"I bet she was vacuuming and found it." I glanced over his shoulder, noticing the garbage at the curb. "Try the trash can."

"Bitch, you try the trash can! I'm not dumpster diving! I'm a wolf, not a raccoon," he whisper-yelled.

"Harvey, I'm coughing every five seconds. She'll hear me. Just do your doggy shift thing—"

"We are *not* making 'doggy shift' a thing. And I may turn into an animal, but I have *dignity*."

"Thursday night is ham and yams night... I bet some good leftovers are going to waste."

"God damn it, you know I'm starving for meat," he growled. I pretended to sniff the air indulgently.

"I think I can smell it. Mmmm, it's probably still warm."

"*I hate you* so goddamn much right now," he said disingenuously, saliva pooling around his gums.

"Du hast, *mich?*" I whispered, taunting him as he undressed.

He snarled as he folded his clothes neatly before shifting into his wolf form and trotting to my mom's driveway. Standing on his hind legs, he tipped over the round plastic can. The lid tumbled off and rolled down the street. The sound of glass bottles clinking caused us both to cringe, and I shushed him from the car. Harvey growled at me, his sass showing through despite his canine appearance. He dragged the bag out of the can and sliced it open with his claws. There it was. The Ouija's cardboard box was shoved in the side of the trash bag, soggy and bent. He pulled it out with his snout.

"Yes," I whispered and turned to get back into the car.

Then he sniffed inside the bag and became ravenous for something deeper in the bag, chomping and licking. I threw my hands up in exasperation. I didn't actually think he would go for the ham. Suddenly, the porch light turned on, and my mother came out in a robe, holding a bat.

"Hey, who's there?" she yelled, trotting down the driveway. Harvey startled, pulling the ham bone out of the bag. He looked between the box and the juicy bone in his mouth, dripping with honey-glazed meat. Realizing it was impossible to carry both with paws and a snout, Harvey shifted back into a naked human. He scooped the box up and ran for it, removing the bone out of his much smaller mouth.

"Oh my God," I wheezed with a shit-eating grin. "This is gold."

All my mother saw was a naked guy running away from her trash bin, with her ham bone in one hand and the Ouija board in the other.

"What the hell is wrong with you? I'm calling the cops!" she screamed as Harvey made it to the car.

"Fuck. Fuck. Fuck. Fuck," he whispered as he threw the door open and jumped in. He tossed the box in my lap and the ham bone on his. I was crouched down so I couldn't be seen. The engine roared to life, and the tires screeched as he pulled a U-turn. My mother ran down the street waving the bat while gravel sprayed toward her.

I was cackling by the time we made it around the corner, barely able to catch my breath and ignoring the sand falling from my mouth. "You're so lucky I didn't have a disposable camera!"

"We will *never* speak of this!" Harvey barked.

"Harv, you have no idea how happy I am that I got to see that before I die."

"Shut up," he said, biting meat off the bone. "I can't believe your mom wastes all this food."

"She doesn't eat a lot of leftovers, and my dad's in a nursing home; she can only bring him so much." My face flattened slowly, and my voice turned solemn. "I'm all she has." That realization took a lot out of me. *If I do survive this, will I ever see her again? Will I ever see Harvey again?*

He snapped me out of my thoughts. "So, where to?"

"There's a compound a county away. It's literally two thousand square miles of undeveloped land and paved roads. We used to go to bonfire parties out there in high school. No one will see us, trust me."

We made it to the deserted compound in under thirty minutes. I slept most of the way, exhaustion setting in. It would have been impossible to see in the pitch-black night if it weren't for the headlights. Harvey cut the engine, leaving the lights on, and we got out. He threw on pants and a belt, trying to avoid clipping his dick in the zipper. I had to admit it to myself, Harvey was well-hung.

I pulled Bane's board out, gently setting it in the middle of the road, keeping the mouse in the pocket of my black JINCO jeans. The headlights made the ivory glow. Harvey grabbed the other board; its box was stained with cooking oils and dusted with lavender Carpet Fresh carpet powder. He gnawed on the ham bone, which was picked clean, and threw the Ouija board down on the cracked pavement carelessly. I shot him a bothered look.

"*What*? Fuck that guy."

"Yeah, but we still need it in one piece for this to work." I fished the mouse out of my pocket, eager to call for Bane. I recited the summoning spell and called his name. I felt a cold breeze from behind before my demon wrapped his arms around me, his silver-blue hand nudging under my tight crop top.

"How are you feeling, my little dream?"

In truth, I couldn't breathe half the time, and I was tired and weak. But I opted to tell him the only truth that would comfort him.

"Terrified," I responded as he gently glided his lips up and down the skin behind my ear.

He stopped. "Are you flirting with me?" I smirked, turned my head to look at him, and nodded. He kissed me gently, stroking my jaw. "Give your friend the planchette."

Harvey walked over, taking the triangle mouse from my hand and staring uneasily at Bane.

"I can only bring one human back, so we need another demon to retrieve you. You will stay with him unless you're needed to guard her. I sent you the modified spell. Do you have it?" Bane asked.

Harvey nodded, tapping the mouse on his temple and fishing meat out of his teeth with his tongue.

"Good. You will summon '*Slater*' with it. We need him in a good mood. Do what he says, and do not piss him off."

Harvey cleared his throat, put the mouse to his lips, and recited the spell,

"Rise, rise, demon of sleep.

"*Slater* comes from the deep.

"Ghost to flesh. Spirit to bone.

"At my side.

"This night alone."

We waited for a moment, and nothing seemed to happen. Harvey looked around and started to ask if he had done something wrong or if he should try again. But something growled in the distance, interrupting him. He turned toward the blazing headlights. Out of the darkness, a tall figure with massive shoulders stepped into view.

The newcomer's skin was a silver-blue like Bane's, but his wavy, jet-black hair sat at his shoulders like Brandon Lee in The Crow. He ran his fingers through the strands on one side, pushing it behind his pointed ear to reveal a crystal plug lined in silver. Where Bane had two spikes in his lower lip, Slater had two hollow, silver gauges the width of a dime, with sharp canines gleaming behind them. His eyes were narrow but had the same piercing blue iris with jet-black sclera as Bane's. And he was naked, cocks swinging around as he walked. He looked like he wanted to kill all of us.

I clung to Bane, who felt a pang of jealousy that another demon scared me so much.

The ham bone slipped from Harvey's hand, and he stumbled backward, chest heaving. Slater stalked forward, his shoulders seeming to roll with each movement. The demon growled like a damn dinosaur. Within seconds, he was inches from Harvey's face, who swallowed hard.

Harvey was muscular and tall, but the demon was twice his width and towered over him by almost a foot. Slater sniffed his neck and then glanced down at the bone, willing it to fly from the ground into his hand. He held it up with a disgusted, questioning look.

"I need meat. I'm... a wolf... I'm hungry," Harvey stated, trying to remain confident.

"You are hungry?" Slater responded quickly with a raspy voice, then threw the bone into the darkness. He lifted a thumb to wipe away excess meat juice from Harvey's mouth. My friend flinched and began to tremble when a sharp claw popped out and sliced a small cut on his bottom lip. "Then we better get you some food, *pup*."

Slater lowered his hands to Harvey's belt, unbuckling it. Harvey, chest rising high and falling deep, tried to block his hand. But the demon froze him. I could spot the terror of paralysis in anyone's eyes. I could smell it, feel it. With much shame, I realized I enjoyed the aura of fear coming off of him. My friend's panic sent chills through my thighs. I was truly turning into a monster.

"That is not your fear to siphon, my love," Bane whispered. "You'll learn to control it over time but try now."

Slater looked down at Harvey, never breaking eye contact as he slid the belt off. He put the strap around Harvey's neck, looping it through the buckle. The demon waited, watching his captive's eyes water. He smirked before snapping the belt tight, strangling him.

I motioned to stop the torture, but Bane held me back. "*Do not move*," he instructed, sounding almost *happy*.

Slater lowered his lips to Harvey's ear, grabbed a fist full of his hair with his free hand, and whispered, "I think you are in need of some training, *pup*. First, I do not want my dog off his leash unless I say so. You stay by *my* side tonight. Is that not what you said when you called me here?"

The makeshift leash loosened as Harvey, finally unfrozen, swayed and gasped. Slater's breath filled his ear. "Take your pants off."

Harvey glanced over at us, pleading and trembling, but Slater grabbed his jaw firmly and forced him to look up.

"No. No. No. You are *mine* now. You do as I say. Take. Them. *Off.*" When Harvey didn't move, Slater tugged the belt tight again, lip twitching. Harvey unfastened his pants quickly. "Good boy." The leash loosened as soon as the denim hit the ground. "Look at me; that's it. Eyes on me. Now, on your knees."

I covered my mouth, but Bane took my arm and held it at my side, reaching into my panties and caressing my center as he made me watch. "I remember when I finally found *you*, my little dream," he laughed in my ear. "Let them have a moment."

Harvey knelt; the demon gripped his hair and held his leash. He was inches away from Slater's cocks and looked at them in shock. That's when I noticed Harvey was getting hard, his knot swollen, with precum beading at the tip. He tried to cover it up but was not successful.

"The second one, grab it. He wants to say hi to his new toy."

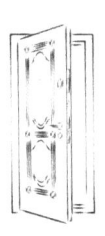

Harvey's cheeks went crimson as he shook his head slightly, but not to say "no." He was trying to shake himself out of a bizarre dream. I could taste his excitement; it was nice but not nearly as good as his fear. He hesitated, and the leash went tight.

Harvey hurried to grab the coiling cock with both hands. It gave him a fight as it twisted against his palm like a snake.

"Nice and tight," Slater instructed.

Still wincing at the tight belt around his neck, Harvey complied, but his grip made the sentient cock strike at him. It was a lot more vicious than Bane's friendly spirit. When Harvey squeezed it tighter, it calmed begrudgingly.

"Good boy. Kiss him." Slater ran his fingers through Harvey's soft blond hair and scratched gently at his scalp. Without hesitation, Harvey leaned forward and kissed the tip. "No. Kiss it like the dog you are."

Harvey swallowed hard, stuck out his tongue, and licked the head of the cock from bottom to top, separating a slit in the tip.

Slater groaned, loosening the leash and letting his shoulders fall. "Good boy. Again. Keep going. Good *boy*. Ssss, again." Harvey was licking the tip repeatedly. The cock became restless. For some reason, I was getting off on watching, and guilt churned in my gut.

"Open wide."

Harvey opened his mouth, and the cock leaped forward like a snake striking. It tried to fit but could hardly make it past the tip.

I flinched and squirmed, remembering how a sentient cock felt inside me. My cheeks flushed as Bane continued to rub my center. My belly tensed with pleasure.

Keeping the leash taut, Slater kept Harvey from retreating with a firm grip on his hair. The cock muffled a yelp as it tried to force its way in again and again. "Open!"

"He cannot," Bane said. "It will take time for his body to adjust for you. Time we do not have, brother. You will have to help him transition another day."

The eager cock was pulled out and tamed with a squeeze. Harvey gasped, hungry for air and shaking but never breaking eye contact with Slater. In turn, Bane pulled his hands from my panties, leaving me eager and restless.

Slater backed up, examining Harvey's large, hard cock and throbbing knot. He smirked, crouching down and gripping it firmly. "Hands at your side. Do not move." He stroked it, tugging Harvey's hips forward. Harvey's brows flinched, and he breathed faster. "You even pant like a pup. Are you going to be a good boy and wear a nice furry tail plug for me?"

Harvey swallowed, furrowing his brow, unsure of what he meant. When Slater's grip on the belt made the leather groan, he nodded anyway. "Ye-yes, sir," he said, failing to stifle a moan. A sheen of sweat coated his flushed skin.

Groaning, Slater rubbed the cock faster and kissed him. Their lips parted, the demon's forked tongue licking every inch of Harvey's mouth. Harvey moaned, hands remaining obediently at his side. He panted as their tongues collided, sucking his lip into his mouth. His cock throbbed.

He moaned louder and faster, tucking his belly as if he was ready to cum. Slater pulled away, letting go of Harvey's cock and digging a knuckle into a pressure point on his thigh. Harvey screamed, sitting on his ankles and arching his back, leg shaking. His approaching climax receded with every second that passed.

The demon laughed, releasing the knuckle and kissing him again, pulling his bottom lip into his mouth. He bit down hard, piercing the skin. Harvey screamed again as blood dripped down his chin. Slater licked it up and kissed him, reaching around to rub the rim of Harvey's ass.

"Oh God..." Harvey whispered, swallowing hard. "Wait..."

He forced a finger in, and Harvey moaned desperately, falling forward into the demon's chest to give him better access. Slater pushed his finger in deeper, and Harvey's mouth opened in surrender.

Slater laughed, putting his lips to Harvey's ear again.

"I am going to edge the fuck out of you until you can take all of me *everywhere*," he said menacingly, smiling and driving his finger in harder. "You are *mine* now."

Precum hung from Harvey's tip, swaying with each thrust. His mouth was open wide as he moaned and pressed his face into Slater's chest, nodding with tears streaming down his crimson cheeks.

Slater pulled his finger free. Harvey looked ashamed and devastated; his entire face was flushed, and his jaw ticked. His eyes were locked on his demon, who stood above him and licked his finger.

"Now shift."

Instantly, panting and stunned, Harvey transformed into his wolf form. His dark silver fur was soft and well-groomed, shining over each defined muscle.

Slater looked pleasantly surprised, even prideful. "You are a fierce werewolf. Heel." Harvey went to his side, obedient and unwavering. "Let us get this fuck dealt with," he said to Bane. "My dog is hungry."

18

BUFFY

We waited on the dark beach in the Dream World for hours, and the Sandman did not show up. The cheap Ouija was laid out in front of us on the white sand, my fingers resting tiredly on the mouse. According to Bane, these cheap boards would summon a demon at random, but if you were the previous user, you could summon the last demon that came through—like a star sixty-nine for Ouija boards. All you needed was a name.

"Sandman..." I croaked for what felt like the millionth time. I hated his name on my lips. He ignored my summoning, and I shuddered, nuzzling my cheek into Bane's lap. We summoned the Sandman exactly as he requested in the contract that he embedded in my skin: using the same crusty board to invite him there with a promise of safe passage onto the beach. As soon as he showed, we were to call off the guards, escort him to the Sacred Sands, and allow him access. But it seemed he wanted to wait until his best bargaining chip—my health—was hanging on by a thread.

Behind us sat the impenetrable cavern containing the Sacred Sands. It was guarded by a hundred demons, several spells, and a large silver gate. My body was significantly weaker, but the scenery and lapping water kept my mind at ease. It was beautiful here, like a dream I'd never want to wake from.

Clothed in a similar cashmere dress to the one I wore the previous night, I sprawled out on the shimmering sand in the moonlight and tried to rest. As luck would have it, having twenty-four hours until I would die didn't mean I would be able to stay conscious for the last day. It was a cruel joke the Sandman snuck in. Bane would have to see me as if I was dead.

My breaths were shallow and quick. My jaw unhinged whenever I gagged or opened too wide. The sand that escaped when I coughed created mounds like ant piles, and I had nothing left to vomit when it made me gag. It was a guessing game when my body would give out. If I had to guess, my time was almost up.

Bane stroked my hair, gritting his teeth. He had already moved my jaw back into place four times and caught every grain from my mouth in his hand. Then he made it disappear so I didn't have to look at it.

"He will pay for this, my little dream. I can not comfort you, but I can promise you vengeance." I was too tired to even nod, let alone tell him he *was* comforting me.

Slater had taken Harvey to the waterline with a bowl of raw meat and ordered him to shift to human form. Judging by the many sounds of satisfaction, Harvey was made to service him, but not before a struggle had taken place.

I coughed again, my eyes watering and bloodshot as I choked on the coarse sand. Bane brushed my hair from my face, tensing and catching the rusty-colored sand again. A tear rolled slowly over the apple of my cheek. I looked at the board and whispered his name again.

"Sand... man."

The wind shifted, and the beach sand scattered across my face. As weak as I was, I would have laid there ignoring how the grit almost blew into my eyes, if I hadn't felt a presence accompanying it. I pushed myself onto my elbows. Wheezing through dry, chapped lips, I looked around for any sign of the Sandman.

"He's close." My voice was nearly gone.

"Slater, it is time!" Bane yelled urgently.

I heard the demon groan and hiss, disappointed that his time taunting his new sex slave had been interrupted. Slater gave an order. Then the pair closed the distance between us; Harvey trotted closely by his demon's side in wolf form. Slater's hard cocks were coated in saliva, precum actively dripping from the tip. Dark blue hickeys and shallow bite marks stamped his thighs and the base of his member.

"What is it, brother?" he asked, glancing around.

The wind blew again, this time stronger. Bane stood up and pulled me to my feet. I swayed, falling against him. He caught me under the arm and held me up.

Harvey whimpered at the sight of me. Slater looked down at him sternly, making my friend bow his head and tuck his tail.

The sand turned orange in front of us, twisting into a cyclone. We squinted our eyes, Bane shielding us with his large arms. Before it could settle, the shadow of a man could be seen behind the spinning orange wall.

"Buffy, right? You look like hell, darling," a familiar voice taunted. Chills ran up my spine as the sand fell to the ground. Bane's lip twitched as he glared at the tall, thin man. His skin was desert orange and dry, and his eyes were antique gold from corner to corner. Dressed in linen pants that looked more like cheesecloth, he grabbed at his dick, adjusting it excitedly. "I have been thinking about you."

My heart dropped, and I looked away.

Bane roared. "Let us get this over with," he said, bearing his teeth at the Sandman. Bane turned to the guards. "You are excused. All of you. Leave now!"

Exchanging looks of reluctance, they did as instructed. Slater walked forward, and the Sandman stepped aside, giving the passing guards a better look at who they were leaving their post vulnerable to. Malice burned in their eyes.

But the Sandman only fixed his golden gaze on Harvey. "A werewolf? Why should I trust it?"

"I have promised you safe passage on this beach. My word is my bond. Slater is the best mage in the Dream World, and I need him. The wolf is his dream," Bane answered. "I will not interrupt his mating haunt. You have taken enough from us." They exchanged tense glances.

I coughed, gagging as a mound of sand poured from my throat. I dug my fingernails into Bane's side as I strained through it. He willed it all to disappear.

As I bent over, gasping, the Sandman leaned forward. "Does it taste the same coming up as it did when you sucked it out of my cock?" Bane lunged for him, and I fell. Harvey caught me on his furry back. "Ah, ah, ah. Safe passage: No harm can come to me, no imprisonment or thrashings, or the girl dies *now*."

"Let us go to the damned sands then," Bane said in a gravelly voice, inches from his face.

He picked me up and threw me over his shoulder. I grabbed the spikes on his back to steady myself from the bouncing of his sulking stomps. Slater and Harvey walked to the silver gate, and after a long ceremonious display of incantations, the spells were broken. Even in the dim moonlight, the silver gate lost some luster. Bane held out a hand, and the doors lifted, nearly flying off the hinges.

He wasted no time charging inside, and the Sandman strolled behind him. I could feel his eyes on me, his thin lips smirking, as I fought to stay awake. Bouncing on Bane's shoulder, I focused on the small of his back and how the last spike fit perfectly in the palm of my hand. I was safe with Bane. Even if he let our worlds succumb to this scumbag, he wouldn't let anything happen to *me*. Selfishly, I took comfort in that.

Slater and Harvey followed behind the Sandman quietly as we walked down the steep cavern steps for a long time. My hacking echoed over the deep walls, and I groaned in exhaustion, my body limp.

"This better not be a trick, demon. I will kill her if I don't see the Sacred Sands soon."

Bane growled under his breath, holding me tighter. His hands clutched the backs of my thighs, practically pulling them apart.

Finally, we came to a large room with ceilings twenty to thirty feet high. The space was lit by blue torches larger than any I had seen. From ceiling to floor was jagged black stone, shimmering like a mine that was rich with silver. A dais platform sat in the center of the room, as wide as a large area rug. The surface was free of a throne or any decoration, and high above it, countless grains of sand of all different colors floated by the ceiling like a funnel cloud that refused to touch the ground. It was magical.

Bane set me down next to the steps of the dais, and I stared at the sand floating ten or more feet above us. It sounded like a rainstick, and it calmed me.

"I'm glad you got to see this at least once," Bane whispered against my forehead, kissing me and stroking my head before standing up.

My hands slipped out from under me, my arms too weak to hold my weight. Bane turned to snarl at our foe. But I just laid my weary head on the cold stone floor, forcing my eyes to stay open. My vision stayed blurry as he walked away. Harvey whimpered again, moving as if he wanted to be by my side.

"Step onto the dais and take your prize!" Slater growled. "Let the girl be free of your curse."

The Sandman stared up in awe at the magnificent sight, ignoring the demon and content with my prolonged suffering. When he finally stepped toward it, Bane stopped him with a large hand against his chest. He got nose-to-nose with the orange spirit.

"Do not forget the bargain. You get what you asked for; she is free of the curse *immediately*. No harm comes to her once they are within your reach," Bane growled, lips shaking.

The Sandman smirked, shoving his hand off of him. "Do not worry, demon. I am done having my fun with your ragged *whore*."

Baring his teeth, Bane turned his shoulder to let the Sandman pass and followed behind him as he climbed the short stack of steps to the dais. Slater moved with Harvey to the other side of the room, admiring the Sacred Sands from across the Dias.

"The black and silver must be bothersome. Perhaps you would

like your filthy sand back, too. I took the liberty of saving every grain she has coughed up," Bane remarked, his footsteps loud as he stomped up the stairs behind him. Without waiting for an answer, he summoned the sand he had collected from my coughing fits. It covered the entire floor, caking up the steps and blanketing the dias.

The Sandman looked around, taking in the mess. "Funny. I do not remember her making me cum this much. In any case, it is an improvement to your *drab decor*. Thank you. I accept your *gracious* gift. Now..." The Sandman stopped on the top of the platform, smiling wide as he held out his arms. "...I will take the sands, bond them to my very being, and have unlimited reign forever," he declared triumphantly. He waited for them to come to him, only they wouldn't move. "*Demon*. We had a bargain. What spell did you fail to lift to keep them from my reach?"

Bane stopped just behind him, snarling. "I have no intention of breaking our deal. To behold power this great, you must respect it; *bow* to it. For once, humble yourself, and you will receive your *Sacred Sands.*"

The Sandman let out a long breath and bowed begrudgingly, facing the thick layer of orange sand Bane had cast to the floor. At the full bend of his bow, golden shackles sprung from the sand and latched to his wrists. He gasped.

"Now!" Bane shouted to Slater. They both lifted their hands. All at once, every grain of the Sandman's cursed orange sand lifted from the floors and steps. It rushed around the vortex of Sacred Sands by the ceiling and down to the shackled spirit. It spiraled violently around his body, forming an hourglass shape.

"Heat! Now!" Slater yelled. The demons' palms glowed molten red, making a pulse of yellow light shake the entire cavern. Heat kissed my face, and I squinted. When my eyes finally adjusted, I lifted my head. I saw it. They turned his cursed sand into a massive, orange-stained hourglass. Gold sealed the top chamber to the cavern ceiling and fused the bottom chamber to the dais.

The Sacred Sands fell from their spinning suspension, filling the top of the hourglass nearly to the brim. The Sandman was trapped inside from the waist up, shackled. The spirit was still positioned in a full bow, bent at the hips, and stuck in the glass wall. It dug into his burnt orange skin, all but cutting him in half. Outside, his waist and legs kicked and writhed. Inside of the glass, his torso and arms flailed and jerked as he screamed.

Slater muttered incantations as he walked in circles around the structure, with Harvey following close behind. With every word, pulses of pink light clung to the glass before disappearing.

"Bane!" the Sandman yelled over the dull chanting. "You are bound to give safe passage on your beach! Release me!"

"We left my beach a long time ago. This cavern is inland. You had your safe passage. But do not fret, Sandman. As promised, the Sacred Sands will be within your reach soon enough," he responded flatly. The sand trickled from the top chamber just inches from the spirit's face. "Of course, you cannot cast magic from within the hourglass, thanks to my mage, so I will manage its power while you are... tied up."

The Sandman yelled and cursed as he tried to break free. Despite his efforts, he could not shift his body into sand.

"Is it not a fun truth, Sandman..." Bane began, coming up behind him and reaching around his waist. "...that you cannot destroy that which is made from your own flesh? This glass is thick and made from the products of your own immortal body. You cannot break it.

It will contain all of your magic. You will *never* escape. It can take *in* more of you, though I think you look comfortable like this."

He tugged the spirit's pants down. "There is one small problem. It is not very soundproof, and I do worry how you may persuade someone to help you," Bane added, grabbing a tight fist of the Sandman's cock and pulling out a silver dagger.

The Sandman screamed and kicked, but nothing could stop Bane from slowly sawing at his length. Black, oil-like blood dripped from the gruesome cut as he screamed in agony. The blade heated red hot, cauterizing the wound and stopping the bleeding. The stench of burning flesh turned my stomach. After a long moment, the cock was pulled free and held firmly in Bane's hand.

"Is this it?"

I coughed, releasing more sand from my mouth; the curse was still alive and well.

"Do not look away. I want you to see this," my demon said, smiling down at me.

The new pile of orange sand hovered over Bane's palm. He stuffed the dick with it until it was stretched to its full length. Then, he worked it through the glass and forced the cock down the Sandman's throat. The spirit gagged and choked, trying to spit it out. But a glass muzzle crept over his face, holding it in place. With a flick of his wrist, Bane broke the Sandman's nose for good measure.

The Sacred Sands continued to fall, reaching the chains that shackled him to the floor. Slater finished the last pink puff of light, completing his spells in the same spot he began. Bane smiled, watching the Sandman's naked ass and legs squirm in terror. I gasped and wheezed, my condition declining rapidly.

"Slater, your pup. He needs fresh meat, does he not?"

Harvey's wolfy jowls dripped with ropes of saliva. "Yes. He is starving, brother."

"He may have his legs, save the skin of his thighs. Let him feast."

The Sandman flailed in panic as he watched the wolf being walked around slowly to his exposed backside.

Bane dropped his silver dagger at the bottom of the stairs and turned to me. "On your back."

My voice was hoarse as I reached for him. Something wasn't right. The curse hadn't lifted. "I can't breathe. Bane, the curse is still—"

He grabbed my feet, dragged me from the steps, and flipped me flat on my back. Instantly, it was almost impossible to breathe. Bane tore my dress to shreds. I gasped for air, trying to grab for him so he would stop and listen. Terror filled my entire soul. He batted my arms away as he stripped me.

"The curse will be over when the last of the Sacred Sands have fallen on his head. Until then, I will mark you *slowly*."

"I can't... breathe." I gasped again, trying to sit up.

He pushed me down, kicked open my legs, and climbed on top of me. "Nor can you *die*. But you're so *fucking* sexy when you're panicking on the brink of death," he said, his lips against my neck.

My face ran hot. I was filled with adrenaline. The nudge of his hard first cock against my entrance made my core prime. The eager flinching of his second cock against my ass made my heart race. I was more terrified than I had ever been, but it only drove him mad with lust. It was the weirdest mix of feelings I ever had. My body was auto-responding in panic, but my brain knew I was safe with Bane. In the thrill of the moment, my trust in his protection compelled me to comply.

"Watch the sand bury him alive while I fuck you. Watch that fuck get mauled by the wolf. Do not look away." I was paralyzed again, save for my mouth.

Taking his time to tease me, tongue and lips caressing my neck, Bane turned my head to the hourglass. I watched as a snarling Harvey, restrained by a tight leash, latched onto the Sandman's calf in a frenzied feeding. A muffled cry echoed from within the hourglass as the meat was shredded from the bone.

"Slower," Slater demanded. Harvey obeyed.

"Do you see what I will do to anyone who touches you? You are safe with me, my little dream. No one will ever touch you again when they see the consequences of hurting what is mine," Bane vowed, kissing my neck and wrapping me in his arms tight as I gasped for air. Why the hell was it so hot when he went all murderous for me?

Dear Satan, who art in Hell, thank you for this man, I mouthed over his shoulder.

"Are you ready?"

"Uh-huh," was all I could get out as my face went crimson.

"We will work on that response another time."

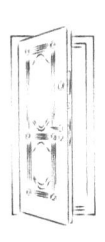

Bane pushed forward hard, and the massive tip of his cock breached my entrance with a pop. The entirety of my pussy burned. His claws unsheathed immediately, raking into the stone floor with excitement. He moaned as he thrust again, impatient for my warmth. My body had changed for him, accepting him with less resistance. But it still hurt to take his length. He pushed, and I yelped.

"Almost there, my love." My nipples tightened in excitement, and my pussy grew wetter.

His second cock cuddled my thigh as it held back for permission to take my ass. But Bane had waited for this moment, and it was for us. I panted shallowly, unable to catch my breath as he shoved himself in deeper, his bulb getting caught over my pelvic bone.

"This might hurt."

He reached down and pressed against the bulb, thrusting forward. With another pop, it scooped under my pelvic bone and swelled inside me. I winced, and a tear fell from my eye as my pussy burned for him. He stroked my breasts and kissed my neck. I moaned weakly, gasping.

Harvey growled and barked as he demolished the last of one leg. He tucked his face in the flaps of skin that housed the thigh meat and ripped out the bones. Slater cauterized the bleeding. The Sacred Sands were nearly to the Sandman's chest; his angry face was beaded with thick, gritty sweat.

Harvey moved to the next leg, waiting for his handler's permission.

"Eat, pup." The feast went on.

Bane was struggling to fit deeper and gripped my shoulders. Moaning and grunting, he pulled me down onto him. If I could move, I would have hit the ceiling. His massive cock was completely inside me. The bulb gave my g spot no escape as it throbbed, expanding and shrinking in pulses. Bane made a sound I'd never forget, exhaling almost vulnerably as pleasure wrapped around him.

He began fucking me hard and slow, and I let out a weak, horse moan. I couldn't replace the breath and broke out into a coughing fit. He groaned as my pussy clamped around him with every cough. His hips slapped against my thighs, jolting them with every thrust. The sand fell from my mouth to the floor, piling high, and I rested my cheek on it in exhaustion. I could hardly breathe, and my vision began to tunnel.

I looked at the hourglass. The top chamber was still a third full. Panic filled my entire body, unable to believe I wouldn't die yet. But I could feel death's presence. Bane moaned louder, his second cock swiping between my cheeks, fighting to enter.

Bane lifted my frozen legs onto his shoulders. "Take her! Take her ass now. Sss," he hissed between his loud panting and groaning. He sounded vulnerable and consumed by pleasure. My eyes went wide. His second cock, slick with my dripping cum, tunneled into my ass. I tried to yelp, but my voice failed. There was not enough air to pass through my damaged vocal cords.

My body jerked as he fucked me, my tits bouncing. I felt the skin of my sides stretch and roll as his second cock buried itself deep, thrashing hard around the swell of his first cock. Bane hollered, throwing his head back in pleasure. My body was full, his cocks fighting for space. I was soaked with cum from thigh to thigh. The euphoria of suffocating lulled me in and out of consciousness. I let out a weak moan, and guppy breathed through the fucking. Pleasure was coursing through every cell of my body. The sound of his immense satisfaction made me dizzy.

The only thing keeping my orgasm at bay was the sound of Harvey finishing off the last leg, crunching on bones and licking the flaps of skin. I tried to tune it out, glancing at the Sacred Sands as my vision blurred again. The Sandman's face was long buried. The top chamber was an eighth full. It wouldn't be long.

I wanted to dig my nails into the floor as I failed to take in air, my body being ravaged by an insatiable demon. My eyelids fluttered. "Bane... I can't... see," I mouthed.

He fell to his elbows and put his lips to my ear, grunting with every thrust. "You're so fucking sexy. Sss. Say it again."

Gasping, I tried. "I can't..." I guppied the last word; no air left.

"Fuck you are perfect. I *love* you," he growled. "Sss. I love you, Buffy."

A tear fell from my eye as my vision gave out. I could feel air against my eyes, but they couldn't see. I could still feel my pussy inching closer to release, hot cum building and ready to burst from me. I had never known such pleasure.

"I fucking love you," Bane vowed again through ragged breaths, fucking me fast. "I will do anything for you." He groaned in my ear as he neared climax.

I was limp, and his palm gently slapped my cheek to wake me. I couldn't do anything. If it weren't for the curse, I'd be dead. I would have been happy to die while he buried himself inside me.

"Oh *fuck*. You are such a good girl. *Fuck*," he moaned, his voice promising release. His second cock went straight, vibrating so violently it grew hot.

Suddenly, my lungs filled with air. I gasped, my vision coming back. I let out a loud moan. Overwhelmed with relief, I came hard. I squirted all over him, splashing clear juice on his abs. I was still frozen, adrenaline coursing through my veins and eagerness seeping from my pores.

"Bane!" I yelled over and over again. My clit pulsed. Every inch of my pussy, inside and out, felt electrified with ecstasy as I came on him.

"That's it. You are doing so well. I love you so much."

"I love you."

He lost control, burying his head in my neck and filling me with hot cum. He roared, cupping my left breast and digging his claws into my skin. They dug deep enough to nick the wall of my heart.

I didn't cry out. While my heart beat against the tip of his claw, I said again through gritted teeth, "I love you. I'll do anything for you. I'm yours."

"Do you accept my mark?" Bane asked in a hurried voice, trying to speak through his orgasm.

"Yes. Please. I'm yours... forever," I whined.

The wounds from his claws didn't hurt anymore. They felt more like a tickle. Our orgasm was long, and he didn't take his claws out, sending a river of cum through me. He was holding my heart on the tips of his fingers, skewered by his talons, as it began to heal around them. It felt like minutes passed before my body was done healing and convulsing.

Finally, he retracted his claws and rested on top of me, tired and breathing hard. He kept his cheek against mine while he caught his breath. "You are immortal now and mine forever. And I am yours, my little dream. I will give you anything. I will worship you."

19

BANE

Slick, sparkling red blood trickled down Buffy's breasts from where I pierced her skin with my claws. The wounds were healing fast. My heart was full, and it ached every time she moaned for me. The moment she accepted my mark, my entire spirit pulsed with gratitude and love, and with that, a fear unlike any I would ever know. I would never let harm befall Buffy again. I could not bear it.

When my orgasm reached its peak, the bulge on the top of my first cock shrunk, and the cum inside of it emptied into her. Her body rocked as I tugged out of her wet little pussy and ass. She leaked a large puddle of my seed, and it splashed on the floor. She was not used to containing a demon's seed. I would help her when it was time for her to carry my litter.

My cocks glistened with our combined pleasure and her lips were swollen and red. I unfroze her, and she moved to sit up. I gently pressed her chest and shook my head. It was time to give her the best gift I had thought of yet. But my little dream was weak, her pussy spotting with blood, and her body still recovering from the curse.

"I will not have you walk, my little dream. Rest."

I scooped her into my arms and carried her to the dais on shaky legs. I sat her down in front of me, allowing her to look up at the magnificent prison while we waited for Slater to finish raping the Sandman. Harvey was in human form again, with Slater's hand pressing him against the hourglass by his neck. He forced the boy to watch as he split the Sandman's ass open, black blood oozing from it with every thrust. Harvey's face was pale with terror as he watched the savagery.

"Should I tear you open, too?"

Harvey lifted his chin and gritted his teeth, breathing heavily.

"No? Then you do as I say. Understand?" Slater said, going nose-to-nose with the young wolf. He nodded reluctantly. "Say it!" Slater yelled, pounding into the Sandman harder.

"Yes."

"Yes, *what?*"

"Yes, sir."

"Good dog. Now rub my other cock until I cum." He released his throat.

Harvey stumbled forward momentarily before walking behind the demon, reaching around Slater's hips and licking his lips nervously.

The spirited cock squirmed when the human's fingers brushed it, and he pulled back for a moment. Then, grabbing it with more confidence, he tamed the spirit inside quickly and began stroking it. Slater sighed indulgently, and Harvey brows flinched up. He looked up at the demon panting in front of him.

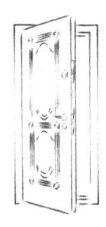

Harvey's cheeks heated, and his breath deepened. "Like that?" he asked, resting his other hand on Slater's hip. He moved his hips forward, hard cock swiping between Slater's cheeks as they nudged him with each withdrawal. He hissed.

"Fuck, yes," Slater moaned, leaning forward to rest his forehead against the glass, providing better access.

The young wolf noticed and brushed his cock against Slater's entrance, coating the rim in precum. He grabbed his hip tighter and breathed deeply, face flushing with arousal as he nudged the tip against the tight hole again.

"Oh fuck..." the boy whispered as his hand twisted up and down Slater's spirited cock, working longer and faster strokes. He rubbed his other palm from Slater's hip to his back, tracing over the sensitive spikes. Slater moaned every time his hand ran over one, and the boy took note, worrying his brow in eagerness. Then he cupped Slater's shoulder and nudged at his entrance again.

"Do you want it?" Harvey asked softly, leaning down to lick a spike. He took it into his mouth and sucked, his lips plumping over the silver.

Pleasure exploded through Slater, molten cum pouring from his spirited cock. The young wolf groaned as he massaged the release over Slater's length. Then he tugged the demon from the Sandman's ass and gently pushed his shoulder down to bend him over. Disarmed by his orgasm, Slater did not fight.

"*Fuck*, I want to come in your ass," Harvey groaned before he took an entire spike in his mouth and tried to push himself into Slater's entrance.

"Oh fuck!" Slater moaned, arching his back and trying to maintain control as he massaged his bigger cock through his orgasm. "What...are you...?" He growled, clearly on the verge of giving in.

I pulled Buffy higher on my lap and wiped the cold sweat from my brow as we watched them finish.

"I never thought I would see the day that Slater would be topped," I whispered in her ear.

"You want it?" the young wolf asked, wrapping an arm around Slater's waist and tugging harder. Eagerly, he thrust his cock against the rim. It stretched over his tip. "Oh God, take it for me," he moaned hoarsely with his lips against the spike, feeling a man for the first time. He sucked at a large spike with passion, flicking his tongue over it and humming with excitement.

Slater grunted fast, spilling cum. His knees nearly buckled before he snapped straight and twisted to grab the wolf by the neck, throwing him down hard. "Lay down and stay still!" He paralyzed him and dropped his knees on either side of the boy's ribs. Slater stroked both cocks as the last of his orgasm spilled over his dream's chest and chin.

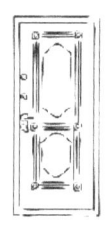

The boy was shaking, terrified of the repercussions, and looking up at his demon with pleading surrender as he finished. Now empty and focused, Slater grabbed the boy's jaw hard and leaned in, seething with anger. The boy scoffed at the crushing pain of his strong grip as their noses brushed.

"*Never* do that again. Do you fucking understand me?"

"Yeah..." He glanced at his demon's lips. "Yes, sir."

Slater flared his nostrils, shaking his head in frustration. He released his chin and stood. When their eyes met, the connection was palpable. For a moment, Slater's rough façade faltered, and he swallowed hard. He puffed out his chest.

"Good," Slater said, his voice deeper than before. "Now shift back and enjoy your new bones on the beach. I will be there in a moment. And if I catch you touching yourself, you will regret it."

Released from his frozen state, the young wolf shifted and ran to the beach with a fresh femur. Slater wiped his cock off with the Sandman's discarded pants, glancing between us and the loose glory hole.

"That boy has you wrapped around his finger," I jested. Slater threw the cloth at my face, and I laughed, balling it up and throwing it down.

"He is *not* a boy," Slater admonished sternly, pausing to admire the carnage. "The guards are going to praise you for this." He nodded to the Sandman's torn ass. "I do not think we will have trouble getting volunteers for rotation anymore. He is *so* fucking tight."

Resting her head on my shoulder, Buffy asked, "What's with his thighs?"

"We have to be certain he does not wiggle his way inside and get out through the hole. I also thought you might want to try your new power, securing the last of him," I explained, gripping her ass and picking her up. It was finally time to give her the best marking gift I could ever conjure. Slater waved us off, heading to the beach to be with his dream.

"I can walk, my love."

"No. You should be carried everywhere, my beautiful demoness."

I settled her down on her knees in front of the massacred ass of the Sandman and kneeled behind her. I was surprised that she did not vomit from the sight. *She is so fierce already.*

"Summon the last of the sand you coughed," I directed, my large hand covering hers to guide it. "It is easy. Just will it."

Buffy did, and it *was* easy. The sand swirled between her and the mangled Sandman. I willed the hanging flaps of skin to open, and they fanned out like bat wings flush against the glass. "You will bond his skin to the glass first, then the sand to his skin. Then add heat, and it will trap his skin in the glass. I will help you."

"I got this," she insisted, refusing my help. She did as I said, easily trapping the skin between layers. They fused entirely within the wall of the hourglass. There was no way for the Sandman to move from the spot ever again.

"Good job. Now..." I was unable to contain my laugh as I pressed her hands against the glass. "...the sand will move to the top chamber by human day and fall by human night, slowly burying him alive over and over again. He will never die, but he will feel like he is suffocating and being crushed under the weight. And he will always feel when someone rapes him, which will be often and brutal. He will be terrified every time. But my gift to you, my little dream..." Our hands glowed for a moment. "...is that you can always feel his terror whenever you will yourself to, as can I. As a demon, you need fear to have pleasure. You will have endless pleasure, an endless reserve of healing energy."

She picked up a shard of bone from the floor, scraping it along the rim of his ass. *She is ruthless.* His body quivered. Her head swayed back in ecstasy, her supple lips parting with a smile. Her new body felt electrified with satisfaction as she willed herself to siphon his terror.

"I remember the night he raped me," she mused and sunk the sharp end into him hard. His cheeks shook and flinched. Buffy giggled, leaning back into me as his terror seeped into her veins. "Now he can feel how I did." Then, after pulling it from him and letting it clatter on the floor, she turned to kiss me.

"Are you satisfied with this vengeance, my little dream?" I asked.

She nodded, cupping my cheek. A tear fell from her eyes. "It's perfect. You are perfect. I love you."

Pride swelled in my chest.

It was always night here, but morning was rising in her world. Although she was now safe to stay with me for as long as I could ever want, her wolf friend had to return. It was draining Slater's power to keep him in the Dream World. If he waited much longer, it could weaken him permanently or even reduce him to a filch. We emerged from the cavern to find them saying their goodbyes.

Sitting on the beach, Slater forced the young wolf to sit in his lap, arms and legs wrapped around him. The demon stroked him and periodically stopped to dig deep scratches on his back so he wouldn't cum. The boy arched his back in pain, but Slater kissed him slowly and passionately, laughing at his game.

"My brother has gone soft. I always thought he would break his partner before he had the chance to mark them. But look at what he has become, and without an ounce of terror left in that boy," I said, shaking my head as I cradled Buffy.

"You have to return to your world, do you understand?" Slater said, releasing Harvey's cock.

"What? Did I...?" The wolf cleared his throat and spoke low. "Did I do it *wrong*? I didn't mean to hurt you. I've never... um. Listen, I can learn." Even in the darkness, I could see tears welling.

"That is not it," he answered with a slight grin.

The whole night, the demon had been demanding and cold, but he clung to the boy tenderly. The young wolf lifted his chin and made to leave his lap, but Slater held him firm.

"Stay—"

"I thought you liked it," Harvey choked out. "If I read that wrong—"

"It is *not* that, pup. This is how it has to be. I will come for you in a few days. Summon me—"

"I can't go back to... you don't understand what it's like there for someone like me."

Slater narrowed his eyes at the boy and nodded regretfully. "Summon me with the Ivory Board in three days. Do not touch yourself while you are gone. I will help you transition. It is going to hurt, and it will take some time, so I need you to be strong. And when I mark you, you can stay. You will be mine forever," he said between kisses, stroking Harvey's jaw.

"I hate you."

Slater swallowed hard and furrowed his brows. He put the Ivory Board in his lap. "Until then, my sweet wolf... *sleep*."

Harvey fell back in a deep slumber. Before he hit the ground, he and the Ivory Board disappeared. Slater's body went slack, and he fell backward into the sand. A tired sigh escaped his lips. Hearing the sand crunching beneath my feet as I approached, he tried to compose himself.

"He is perfect," Slater murmured, trying to make his voice deeper than usual. He looked up at us. "He is beautiful, strong, *obedient*. And he is an amazing wolf." He clutched a fist over his heart and swallowed hard.

"He's a good guy. I'm glad you have each other," Buffy said, smiling.

"You are bonding with a human without terrorizing him. He even clings to you. What the hell keeps you so hard for him if he is unafraid of anything?"

Slater scrubbed his face and stood. "I need to mark him quickly. Show me what I need to do. Show me everything."

He walked past us, heading to the main cave. With Buffy wrapped up in my arms, I summoned the guards.

"Let us go *home*. You need rest, and I still have a small gift for you," I said as I carried her back to our moon.

20

BANE

My little dream slept peacefully for three human nights. She was not accustomed to being naked so often. At first, I let her have her way, allowing her to wear the sheer dress. But on the fourth night, I demanded she discard the dress in common areas. Fear crawled up her body as she stood naked in front of everyone, her skin flushed. If she tried to cover herself, I threatened to make her cum in front of them.

I demanded she sleep naked. Sleep was our most sacred pastime and the most fertile moment. She could sleep as often as she wanted, wherever she wanted, as long as she was with me and only me.

Buffy tried to cover herself with her small arms and failed; my eyes devoured every curve. She was upset with me and crawling onto the far side of the bed, pouting and pulling the covers up. I touched her shoulder, and she shrugged me off, hugging herself in shame. Her body was warmer than usual, and I knew it was time. I smirked, pulling her tiny body to me. She huffed.

"Sooner than later, you will be rid of embarrassment and see yourself how I see you. You are perfect and should not feel the need to hide any part of you."

"I should be able to do it on my own terms, Bane."

"You are a queen. You must exude confidence. If I left it to you, you would stay clothed forever."

"I'm confident when clothed."

"And you will be confident naked." I kissed her neck, and the faintest smile broke through her grouchy demeanor. She tried to brush me off, but I kissed her neck again. *"Won't* you be, Queen of Terrors?" I asked, squeezing her breasts. They were firmer than normal, confirming that her body was ready.

"Yes," she grumbled, rolling her eyes and trying to turn away from me.

"You will sleep on your back tonight," I said, smiling.

When she ignored me, I grabbed her by the arm and turned her over. As soon as I had her on her back, I pressed my palm over her forehead and put her to sleep. Her eyes darted under her eyelids as she dreamt. Her body was still, her breathing steady. My face felt hot with need.

I pulled the blankets down and ran my hand over her chest, groping her aggressively. A sleepy groan escaped her lips. I leaned down to take her nipple in my mouth. Asleep or not, her body responded to me, and her breasts tightened under my cold tongue.

She squirmed and adjusted, unable to wake. My heart raced at the sight of her limp body, becoming eager for me while her mind was oblivious. I reached down, rubbing her clit with my thumb as I tugged at her taut peak with my fangs. Her juices soaked my fingertips. *I knew she liked being naked in front of everyone,* I thought with a laugh. *So stubborn.* I licked her tits from bottom to top. Then, pushing them together, I sucked at either side of her cleavage.

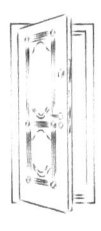

My cocks were painfully hard, the bulb swollen with my seed. I traced my lips down her body as I rubbed my first cock. She groaned as I kept sucking and nipping below her navel. Her body ached for my tongue in her pussy.

I pushed her knees wide and stroked myself for a long moment. She looked like such a little slut, her center glistening for me, and she did not even know. I could not wait to do as I pleased with her while she lay there sleeping, her legs open for me to take my pleasure. She turned her head and let out a small moan that was enough to make me buckle. I fell to my elbows between her legs.

I kissed her clit slowly, and she let out a sleepy moan. I brought my tongue to her entrance and extended it inside of her, circling her depths and licking every ridge along her walls. I could taste her need building, ready to coat my cock. Her lips parted, and she let out a heavy, quivering breath, tits shaking. She turned her head again, brows slightly furrowing. I wondered what she was dreaming of to make sense of the pleasure. I fucked her with my tongue as her hips squirmed subconsciously. She pouted, almost confused.

I pulled out. My tongue parted her lower lips until it met her clit. The fork of my tongue hugged the tiny bundle; I left no part of it unsatisfied as I made short, slow flicks. My lips wrapped around it, sucking and releasing over and over. My chin was dripping. I only stopped when she was ready to cum. I would not let her finish, spending time kissing her thighs as she whimpered and settled.

When she stopped stirring, I did it again and again. My little slut was soaked from thigh to thigh.

Her body was more than ready to receive me. After a few hours of toying with her little pussy, I kissed it one last time and then crawled over her to take my pleasure. I cupped her jaw to rouse her, shaking it gently to see the depth of her sleep. She barely responded. My breath hitched in excitement as I adjusted my cocks. I gave her cheek a couple of quick, gentle slaps, and she groaned, her head falling to the side. I hissed, lining my hard length up.

She was a demoness, but her pussy had not been stretched since the night I marked her. She had to heal. This was going to hurt her so sweetly.

My spirited cock coiled for her. "Not tonight. This is special." It rubbed itself against her thigh instead. Unable to wait another minute, I pushed my cock in forcefully. My heart pounded against my chest as she let out a tired cry, wincing.

"Oh fuck. I'm going to have so much fun with you," I growled through gritted teeth as I popped my swollen bulb into her. She winced again, moaning painfully in her sleep as it doubled in size. I panted in response, impatiently excited. There was no escaping me now; even if she woke and tried to get away, my cock could not be removed until she let me empty my bulb of seed into her completely.

Blinded with excitement, I ravaged her little cunt, pounding into her. She lay there, bouncing under me with her legs spread wide and her tight little pussy wrapped around my cock. Her pussy lips blanched from the stretch. My cock glistened with her need.

Pulling her hips onto my lap, I pressed my body against hers. She sank into the mattress under my weight and groaned as I angled my fat cock upward inside her. A tear fell from her eye, and I growled into her neck.

My lips went to her ear. "You will always be my little fuck toy, you hear me?" I hissed, wrapping my arms around her waist to hold her in place as I rammed myself into her. The sound of her juices easing my thrusts drove me mad. Her moaning picked up. Her chest heaved as her pussy started to spasm around me. Her heavy eyes struggled to inch open, and she tossed her head to the other side. I allowed her to barely wake up so she could realize what was happening to her and make her scream for me.

"What are... you...doing?" she mumbled before her breath caught in her throat, cut off by a hard thrust.

"I will fuck you when I please. Your pussy is mine. Cum for me, you little slut."

She whimpered, unable to find the strength to move her body, apart from her arm lifting for a brief moment to scratch me before falling back onto the bed. She was slipping in and out of consciousness. Her inner walls spasmed tighter, and I fucked her harder, chasing my own release.

"Is this my fucking pussy?" I asked, grabbing her jaw tight and rousing her just enough to answer me.

"Yes..." she muttered, her head lulling.

"That's right. And I am going to squirt my cum in your pussy now. Go back to sleep."

Her eyes fell shut with a gasp. Her only movement was her pussy pulsing around my cock and her belly shuddering with pleasure. She moaned weakly, and my pleasure took over. I came hard, flooding her instantly. I fucked it into her again and again, making sure my seed was deep and coating every inch of her womb. I growled and panted for a long moment as my orgasm carried on. Our orgasms were never quick, and this one lasted longer than most. I could hardly breathe by the time it waned.

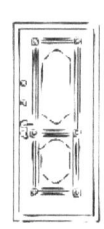

In the last few moments of our pleasure, I woke her. Her eyes and mouth flew open as she threw her head back, confused at her abrupt ecstasy. She whined and moaned for me. As soon as it was over, I froze her, leaving her legs wide and her hips propped on my thighs.

"Bane... what are you doing to me?" Buffy's words were breathless.

"Giving you my litter, my little dream." I pulled myself carefully from her sore pussy. Her hips remained elevated on my lap, and I pressed my palm over her entrance, forcing her to contain all of my seed. I would make sure it took root in her womb.

"Litter? What...?"

"Your body is warm, and your breasts are firm. You will spawn children for us, my love," I explained, smiling and breathless. Pride filled my chest at the wondrous gift I had filled her with.

"Children? Bane..."

I smiled down at my dream, caressing her cheek with my free hand. "You will be a perfect mother to our beautiful spawn. They will be our little terrors." Panting, she nuzzled into my palm. She seemed lost for words and knitted her thin brows. "Remember when I marked you? I said I have a gift for you, Mother of Terrors," I said, failing to hide my excitement. I reached under her pillow and retrieved the blood crystal gauges. "I made these from the sand you bled onto when I carved into you the first time."

I popped a gauge loose with my free hand and pushed a red crystal one in. She cringed slightly as it stretched her lobe wider. I traded hands, keeping her hips balanced on my lap, and did the same to her other ear.

"Do you like them?" I floated a crystal mirror behind my shoulder so she could admire them while seeing herself spread out under me.

"They're beautiful," Buffy murmured with a tear traveling down her cheek.

I worried my brows at her. "What is wrong, my little dream? Does your pussy ache too badly?"

She shook her head and sniffled. Finally, her eyes met mine. "My mother has always wanted grandchildren. I miss her. I worry about her." She sobbed, her face souring. "I always thought she would meet them, that they would grow up with her. I just can't imagine doing this without her."

I wiped her tears away. "Slater is being summoned by his wolf tonight. I will get his help and make this right, my love."

"You would do that for me? Let me see my mom?"

"I will find a way for her to be with our family. I will do anything for you."

"Anything?"

"Of course."

"Next time you want me to spawn our terrors, we need to plan it first."

"This is a gift... but if it is important to you, yes. I will tell you when we should spawn our little terrors... next time."

She laughed and sniffled again. "Okay. Will you unfreeze me now?"

I smiled at her, rubbing my soaked palm in circles over her entrance. She was overflowing with my cum, and I could hear it lapping at the walls inside of her. "No. Not yet. Your womb must drink all of me first for this to work. If you are okay with my spawn taking root?"

Buffy nodded.

"Good, I like you like this," I said, caressing her body with my free hand.

We talked into the night, laughing and kissing. Despite her demand, she seemed excited to spawn. Eventually, she dozed off by herself. She was the sleepiest demoness to ever exist in the Dream World. I smiled at her; she slept in front of me so freely. It was all I could do not to ravage her again. But I needed to let her body rest as my seed searched for a proper place to burrow.

"I love you, my little dream," I murmured, her pussy still cupped safely in my hand. I pulled it away, and only a small amount was left to trickle out. I caught it with my finger and swiped it in her entrance before lowering her hips to the mattress. I laid on top of her body, the tip of my cock plugging her shut to keep our spawn safe, and I fell into a restful sleep. I slept deeper than I ever had. And for the first time, I dreamt of someone other than Buffy. With her were the precious new terrors nesting inside her belly.

BUFFY, QUEEN OF DREAMS

2 years later:

I hid in the shadows of her kitchen, watching her wash the last of her dishes. She wore fuzzy pajama pants with little lambs and a soft cotton shirt. The sun was almost set, but her shades were drawn enough that I could creep closer if I wanted to. But I wanted to wait for the opportune moment. She yawned deeply and shook the dishwater off of her fingers. Then, she started organizing the sponges.

Bane kissed the point of my ear, gently holding my waist. I could feel him smiling. I held back a laugh and nudged him with my elbow. He loved to watch me haunt. I was getting better at it, drawing out the different tactics and building suspense in my victims. But this one was going to be quick and delicious.

She wiped her hands on her pants and turned around, walking right for us. I waited until she was within reach.

"Hello," I said in a menacing growl before jumping out of the shadows and grabbing her. She screamed, jumping up and down and spinning as my arms tightened around her waist. I let out a hearty laugh. "Rawr, I'm gonna get you!" I laughed harder, and she swatted me away.

"You little shit!" she hissed, smacking my arm hard. "Damn it, Buffy, I nearly peed my pants. Stop doing that."

"Sorry, Mom. I couldn't help it," I giggled, throwing my arms around her. "I missed you."

"Yeah, yeah. Where is my son-in-law?" She pushed me out of the way, walking briskly toward Bane. Thankfully, he wore shorts while visiting. "Oh! There he is. Hello, my dear." She wrapped him in her arms and squeezed him tight. Bane hugged her back, picking her up off the ground and swinging her side to side. She squealed with delight.

"Hello, mother of Buffy. Your fear smells exceptional today."

She laughed as her feet returned to the floor. "Oh, that's just the apple pie. I saved you some. Come on now!"

"Mom, we don't really eat human food, remember? It upsets our stomachs."

"Nonsense. He can taste it and spit it out if his tummy hurts. Come on now, Bane," she insisted, shoving him toward the table and urging him to sit. She hurried to the oven, grabbed her mitts, and pulled out a steaming cinnamon apple pie. She was at his side in no time, cutting a slice and moving a forkful toward his mouth. I glanced at an old magazine covering a story of missing people in our town. Skeeters face was plastered across it, my picture a small bubble to his side.

As darkness enveloped the room, a scream echoed from my mother's bedroom. There was a crash, as if something had been hurled at the wall. Incomprehensible shouts became more agitated by the moment, and the three of us exchanged concerned glances. Bane went to stand, but I put my hand on his shoulder.

"I'll take care of it, my love. It will be less scary if he hears a familiar voice," I said, walking past them and toward the room.

"We will meet you there soon, my little dream," he replied, kissing my hand before I slipped away.

My mother swooned with admiration, smiling and raising her shoulders in excitement.

"That is so sweet, Bane. '*My little dream.*' How precious is that? She better be taking good care of you. Now open up." Her voice became more distant, but the fawning was loud and clear. "Do you know how hard it is not to brag about my son-in-law to my friends? How do I explain that you only ever dreamt of *her?*"

The screaming got louder as I crossed the threshold into the bedroom. Dad had Sundowners, a condition some dementia patients get that make them abruptly more aggressive and confused as the sun goes down. Despite his worsening condition, Mom decided to care for Dad at home, so long as I would visit every night to help him rest. The TV remote zipped past my head, and I dodged it easily with catlike reflexes.

"Get the hell out of here!" Dad screamed. "You rotten bitch!"

"Oh, now that's not nice," I said sweetly, hiding my frightening form in the darkest shadows of the room. "Why don't we take a nice nap together?"

"Who the hell are you?"

He swung his arms as I approached. "Daddy, it's me, Buffy, you're daughter."

"Turn on the light! I can't see a damn thing."

I sat on his bed, seeing him clutch his sheets to his chest. He was afraid, but I would never feed off of it. Not my dad's fear, not when he was like this. "Daddy, can I have a hug?"

I reached out slowly, testing his boundaries. He allowed me closer, and I cupped his ears in my hands.

"*Sleep*," I whispered. He fell backward onto the mattress, but I didn't let go. I moved forward and took us to the Dream World. Our bodies fell through the mattress, and the night sky rushed past us, turning to shimmering crystal. We landed softly on the couch in my living room, a new addition to our crystal-moon home. "Is that better, Daddy?"

"Oh, sweetie. I'm so sorry. Did I hurt you?" he asked, his eyes free of the cloudiness of dementia.

"No! No. You were just about to hug me, actually," I reassured, latching onto him. He hugged me tightly, rubbing my back.

We jolted as the room shook, a crystal-shattering boom echoing around the space. I pulled away from my dad's embrace and turned.

"My love, can you please work on a softer entry? You cracked the floor again," I scolded Bane. He had my mother in his arms, who was still attempting to shovel a fork full of steaming pie in his mouth.

"I will fix it," Bane said, the new pie chunk in his cheek.

He set my mom down, and she quickly turned to my father, who sprung up from the couch. They embraced each other, her trying not to drop the pie tin and him trying to smell it from over her shoulder.

"Was I okay today? I wasn't too much, was I? I'm a little fuzzy on the details, but I may have called you a terrible name," Dad asked, his head hung low.

"No, honey bun, you just need to drink more water when I tell you to, that's all." She smacked his hand as he tried to pick at the pie. "Save some for the kids!"

"Mom, no. The kids cannot have human pie. They're in their terrorizing twos. The sugar will have them throwing you through the crystal wall."

"Oh, you're no fun. Where are my grandbabies, anyway?"

There was a knock at the door, and Slater came through with our five little bundles of ferociousness. They hung off his limbs and crawled over his back, claws digging into his thick skin.

"I have come to transfer your spawn to their grandsires," Slater grumbled, reaching over his shoulder to grab Lillian from his back. She giggled as he set her down. Like her siblings, the demoness was small, dark blue, and had her father's eyes and ears. They only wore white cloth diapers and had not yet grown into their silver spikes, but their baby fangs were like tiny needles.

Lillian had a pink bow on her head where a small tuft of straight onyx hair grew out. Phillip had the same tuft, pin straight and slicked back, but without a bow. Tommy only had a few black curls sprouting from his mostly bald head, while Chucky had a wild mane of untamable raven locks. Angelica, the oldest of the litter, had short black pigtails and was the most rambunctious and defiant of the five.

Lillian caught sight of my mother, and her face lit up. She ran full speed to her, drawing the attention of the other kids, who quickly abandoned their maiming of Slater to ambush her, too.

"Gah-maa!" they all yelled as their feet pitter-pattered toward their grandma.

"Claws away! Claws away!" I reminded them as they reached for her and crawled up her leg. Luckily, they only penetrated the fleece fabric of her pajama bottoms this time. They retracted their claws, falling on their diapered butts and reaching up for her.

"What am I, wood?" Dad asked, waiting for his hugs. Chucky and Angelica knocked him over as the others crawled all over Mom, who was now seated on the couch. Dad struggled to slide his way onto the couch, too.

"They are all yours," Slater declared, wiping his brow and eyeing the pie with interest. He poked a finger in and tasted it, humming.

"Slater, I sure am happy to see you again, buddy. But I wish you would wear some pants," my father remarked, trying to keep his eyes anywhere but on the demon's massive junks, which were barely hidden under a loincloth. My mother laughed but kept her attention on tickling Phillip's belly. He giggled loudly and rolled around on her lap.

"We do not have *'pants'* here, old one," Slater replied before eyeing Bane's short white bottoms with distaste. My dad furrowed his brows at the casual mention of his oldness.

"Okay, you all have fun. We've got it from here," my mother said without taking her eyes off the kids.

"Are you sure you guys are okay with watching them alone?" I asked. "They're really figuring out the scaring thing lately."

"RAWR!" Tommy growled in the cutest little voice.

Mom pretended to be terrified, widening her eyes and throwing her hands up in surrender.

"Oohh, no! You *scared* me!" she screamed theatrically. Tommy burst into shrieks of joy, clapping. "Oh please, Buffy. They take twelve naps a day and hardly ever poop. You were worse. A poop machine, Bane. She was a *poop machine* as a kid!"

"Okay! That's enough. Let's go," I said with red cheeks. "Don't forget to brush your fangs."

"Are you sure you two have enough power reserved to keep us for the whole night? I heard one of your little friends say it drains you sleep-folk to bring mortals here," my dad asked as I made my way through the kids, kissing and hugging each of them goodbye.

"We have a... stash of sorts, an endless stream of terror. So don't worry. You aren't hurting us," I assured him as I kissed the last of my spawn.

"Be good, my little terrors," Bane said as he cupped their cheeks and kissed their foreheads. They looked up at him, doting. "If your grandsires speak well of you, I will bring you the frozen tears of our enemies for dessert."

The kids cheered and began running amok as we followed Slater out of the portal door and into the main cave. We removed our human clothes and hung them on the rack.

"Will you be joining us tonight?" Bane asked Slater as we descended the stairs, noting the deep knees each member of our court took in our presence.

"I will not, old friend. I would not dare interrupt your anniversary. Besides, I have a dog to uncage," he stated, smiling. He took a deep knee, nodding smugly before turning toward his quarters.

Bane and I traversed the tunnel to the beach passing the garden of marijuana he planted. His heelers mutated the strain to thrive in our moonlight, and it grew with fuzzy, purple and pink hairs sprouting around the flower. The pedals looked as thought they were coated in sugar. When smoked, it made a demons dream more vivid, giving them clues about where to haunt. Since growing the herb, there had been more demons finding their human dreams in the past couple years than in the last five centuries combined.

The endless night swallowed us as we walked toward the cave of Sacred Sands. I glanced at the crystal moon to see if I could spot my mom sneaking the kids human food. But from so far away, it was useless, so I turned my gaze to Bane. A scar ran down his neck and chest, and I was reminded of how much we had been through since we first met. The turn of the century, or "Y2K," as humans back home called it, had not been kind.

"How are you managing the dream laws, my love?" Bane inquired.

"It's going alright. Well... you know a caeluman child back home has been dream-projecting. Well, not back home per se, but around Spain in the hidden Sky Realm. He's a young prince, and he's been playing pranks on his father in his sleep since he was in his mother's belly."

"Yes, I have been hearing about the little Prince Nahveal for years. You should haunt him and remind him that meddling in dreams is adult business."

"You're advising me to haunt a minor? He's only a kid. We aren't bogeymen."

"He is not respecting rules, which are clearly laid out in his teachings, and our bogeymen have failed to reign him in. He is very powerful. This behavior could make the king go mad and start wars again. *Haunt* the boy. Frighten him enough to stop his mischief until he is mature enough to wield that power."

I smiled and shook my head. As a mother, I wasn't thrilled about haunting a child, but I would handle it gently.

"Are you going to tell me the surprise yet?"

"No, my little dream. You will see when we get there."

Bane covered my eyes as we entered the cave where we kept the Sandman. He was still there, a shriveled mess of a man, slowly being buried alive again. It didn't matter that Bane kept my eyes shut. I could feel the spirit's fear vividly from across the room. But there was something else in here. I heard muffled moans and wet sounds. Bane guided me across the room and up the steps, then leaned down to my ear. "Are you ready?"

"Yes?" I said nervously. He waited a moment so he could taste my angst a little longer. Then he dropped his hands from my eyes.

We were at the top of the dias, looking at the room below. In front of us were a hundred or more demons having a massive orgy. My cheeks flushed.

Bane pushed me, and I windmilled forward, landing on the top step. If he hadn't grabbed me by the back of the neck, I would have tumbled down the stairs. He turned me to face him and forced me to my knees, shackling my wrists to the floor with long chains. Standing in front of me, his cocks hardened just inches from my face. His sentient cock grazed under my chin, lifting it so I was looking up at my demon.

"Tonight, you will be pleased by every unmatched demon on duty." He grabbed a fist full of my hair and traced the head of his cock over my lips. "Once you say 'go,' they will not stop until they have all spilled their cum inside of you. I will not stop them. I will not allow your mouth to be empty long enough for you to utter the word 'stop.' Whenever you are ready, my little dream, say the word."

Cum beaded at the head of his cock. My center heated. Bane knew how much I loved the idea of having a train run on me. As possessive as he was, I never thought he would allow another demon to take me. But now my hands were chained to the floor as I leaned my naked body forward on my knees with my ass exposed to the line forming below us.

"Are you sure? Bane, you don't have to—"

"Are you my little slut?"

I melted. My mouth watered. The demon behind me rubbed my shoulder, waiting for my signal. He worked a knot out of the muscle, and I moaned. It was a rough week raising five demon toddlers and ruling the Dream World. I needed this.

Another demon stopped at my side, rubbing my breasts, which had been bitten raw from feeding our fangy children for so long. My nipples were sore and aching, and my breasts were several cups larger and heavy with pearlescent milk. It felt incredible when the demon relieved them of their weight, cradling them in his frigid hands and massaging them gently. Silver-white liquid dripped from my nipples as he squeezed them. I groaned as the pressure released.

Someone laid on the ground, trailing kisses up my inner thigh. He kissed my pussy lips, and my thighs heated. I became eager. The line behind me grew long as countless demons, all ready to serve their queen, kneeled and stroked themselves in preparation. Their bulbs were swollen and throbbing for me.

Bane pulled a shard of femur bone from the floor and scrapped it along the Sandman's ass. His terror filled me, and I moaned, throwing my head back. But Bane held my hair tighter, shaking me out of the trance and making me look at him. He smirked at the milk dripping from my chest.

"When you say 'go.'"

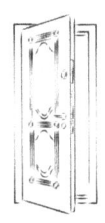

"Go," I commanded. The demon at my back leaned me forward quickly, lining his cock up to my pussy. He wrapped his arm around my waist and tugged me close so I couldn't pull away, and my chains clanked. Bane pulled my jaw down hard, unhinging it wide enough to fit his massive first cock. He shoved the length down my throat, making my mouth and neck stretch over him like a snake eating a mouse. Bane and the demon thrust inside at the same time and fucked me hard from both ends.

I hardly had time to catch my breath as my demon fucked my face. Tears smeared mascara down my cheeks as he drew out his pleasure. Meanwhile, demon after demon pumped themselves into me, their bulbs swelling to twice their size once they plunged inside. Letting them fuck me feverishly and finish was the only way to get them out.

My knees burned as I was taken viciously by an endless string of demons spilling their massive loads deep into my center. I lost count after fifty-six demons, but it continued for much longer. I lost count of how many times I came. It took several hours of demons railing my pussy, licking my clit, and sucking milk from my nipples before the line was down to one.

When the last finished, Bane demanded they line up again to take my ass. I whimpered, my knees bloody and sore in the puddle of juices collecting under me. He pulled out of my mouth, released my chains, and threw me on my back. Before I knew it, my legs were over my shoulders, shackled to the ground beneath me. My ass was wide open for the line of demons waiting for the signal to fuck their second load into my asshole with their sentient cocks.

With my jaw still unhinged, I couldn't protest. Bane straddled my head, guiding his cock into my mouth again. On all fours, his hand tucked under my head, he began fucking my face harder. Since I was an immortal, he gave little concern for my ability to breathe. But the fear of suffocating still coursed through me from my time as a human. His cock swelled with excitement.

"Go!" Bane growled.

Without hesitation, the demons descended upon me, taking turns fucking my ass like rabid beasts. Their sentient cocks thrashed, bucking me hard. This was their second orgasm, and it took even longer for each to finish. My ass burned and ached before the first man was done with me.

I couldn't see any of the demons touching and fucking me. They worked in teams of two or three, holding my hips still and sucking my clit as I was railed. Occasionally, someone would pump fingers into my sore pussy, or spit on it. A puddle of semen splashed under me and ran down the stairs as I overfilled. My body couldn't contain all of it. The puddle flowed halfway down the line, and the cave floor was saturated.

"That's a good little slut," Bane would praise as he fucked my mouth slower, drawing out his pleasure and saving it for the very end.

Finally, the last demon was fucking me, and his sentient cock was taking its time. My pussy and ass were tingling with heat and numbness. Bane pulled himself from my mouth, releasing the chains so my legs fell into the hands of the demon behind him.

Stroking himself, he snapped my jaw back into place. My chest heaved as I watched him rub himself faster.

"Tell me what a little fuck toy you are," Bane moaned, panting. After having his cock in my mouth for hours, I didn't know if I could speak. I tried, but it came out as an incomprehensible garble. He laughed with excitement, gripping my hair and yanking my head toward the head of his cock. "Try again."

"Aye ahma..." I tried again, but my lips were too numb, and my jaw felt like liquid. "Suuhd."

"You sucked so much cock you can not even speak," he growled, biting his lip and stroking faster. He grabbed my hands and made me stroke his sentient cock. Tiredly, I did my best to please my demon. He watched my body bounce as the demon fucking my ass chased his orgasm. "You like getting fucked like that?"

"Ayeah," I mumbled, nodding eagerly. My face was pink and glistened with sweat and saliva. Cum lept from his cocks and coated my face and chest. He growled loudly as he painted his massive load all over me. The demon in my ass rubbed my clit, and I soon followed Bane's release, clenching around his cock. He came hard with a rush spurting deep into my ass. The three of us came for a long minute. My face and chest were completely covered in Bane's cum, and I stuck my long tongue out to lick whatever I could reach.

When we finished, the demon withdrew from my ass, guided my legs gently to the floor, and joined his kneeling companions as they waited for me to recover. Bane lifted me into his arms. Cum splashed on the ground as it poured from my ass and pussy and dripped from my chest and chin. I couldn't open my eyes. Bane stomped through the thick puddles of cum and milk as he took heavy steps to the exit.

I was limp, and my head fell back as I drew in ragged breaths. Cum was still falling from my body as we stepped onto the beach. The crystal moon made the liquid sparkle in the darkness. Finally, we arrived at the water. It was freezing. I shivered and gasped as we submerged, but it dulled the pain.

Bane washed me, letting the inflammation ice down. When I was good and numb and all the cum was removed, he held me close. With my soaked hair slicked back, he kissed me passionately, cradling my head. Despite the frigid cold, I was too exhausted to open my eyes or hold my head up.

There was a drop off against the shore, like a wall of sand. Bane leaned my body against it and rested my head on the beach. With my body still submerged in the water, he took me slowly and gently for another long hour, watching me lull in and out of consciousness. He loved that.

"Wake up, my little dream," Bane whispered lovingly. My eyes fluttered open. "Eyes on me. Don't look away."

He pushed inside deep and emptied himself into me one last time, letting out soft, breathy moans. He was shivering and twitching. With each thrust, my wet chest peaked over the waterline, my nipples tight and hard in the moonlight. In the icy water, his cum felt hot, and I moaned as it poured into my womb and warmed my core. My teeth chattered as I cried for him, my legs spread open as I melted into his heat, inviting it to flood my body.

When he was done, he held me against him and waded toward one of the boils, a patch of bubbling water where the heat of the world's core escaped into the sea. It was warm and rolled against my muscles like a hot tub.

I moaned into Bane's neck.

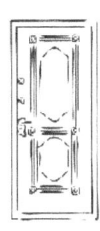

"Mowe," I begged with a jaw like jello.

"More? No. Not too close, my love. It is too hot."

I groaned sleepily and let the rolling water soothe my aching body. When my demon carried me out, he dressed me in a white cashmere dress like he did when I first arrived in the Dream World.

He conjured a white cloth that he pitched over us as a tent. It billowed in the wind to reveal the turbulent water and crystal moon. But it covered us enough so no one else could watch me sleep. Bane kept that for himself.

"A small gift, my love," he said, slipping a silver band over my ring finger. It was set with a massive marquise-cut crystal from the moon. I could hardly open my eyes to see it. "You always dreamed of a human wedding and human things. Now you have a ring to remind you that you are my wife in every world, forever."

I smiled and nudged my chin toward him. He lowered his lips and kissed me.

"Aye..." I tried, but my mouth was still too sore.

"I love you, too, my dream," Bane vowed, laughing.

I nuzzled into him. We slept in the sand, under the stars, the crystal moon, and the flowing fabric as the cool breeze dried us. Wrapped in each other's embrace, we dreamt of each other and the growing family we were spawning. We ruled this way for millennia.

THE END

AFTERWORD

If you or someone you know has been abused or assaulted, please reach out to one of the following programs.

National Domestic Violence Hotline
    800-799-7233

National Sexual Assault Hotline
    800-656-4673

ACKNOWLEDGMENTS

Thank you to my husband for supporting my writing career. He doesn't know how dark this book is, but I'm sure he would still be proud because he is my biggest cheerleader. Thank you to my alpha and beta readers for your excellent feedback, which helped make this work the best it could be.

ALSO BY NANDER

Opals & a Nimbus The Nimbus Series Book 1 (May 2024)

Opals & a Nimbus Official Cookbook (May 2024)

The Nine Lives of Love (Expected July 2025 and also seen in the Shrek Anthology)

Oceans & a Nimbus The Nimbus Series Book 2 (Expected 2025)

ABOUT THE EDITOR

Samantha Swart is a seasoned developmental editor with a passion for crafting captivating romance stories. She has honed her skills in guiding authors to shape compelling narratives that resonate with readers. Specializing in the romance genre, Samantha possesses a keen understanding of the intricate dynamics of love, passion, and relationships. Her editorial expertise extends across various subgenres, including contemporary romance, fantasy romance, romantic suspense, and paranormal romance. Samantha's collaborative approach to editing involves working closely with authors to enhance character development, plot pacing, and emotional depth. She excels in identifying areas for improvement while preserving the unique voice and vision of each author. Outside of her editorial work, Samantha enjoys immersing herself in the world of literature, exploring new romance novels, and staying abreast of emerging trends in the publishing industry. As a true romantic at heart, she believes in the transformative power of the romance genre. www.samanthareadsspicy.com @SamanthaReadsSpicy

ABOUT THE AUTHOR

Born and raised in Florida, NANDER has worked as an ICU nurse, activist, social media influencer, and union organizer. In early 2023, she reconnected with her passion for reading and writing as a means to cope, finding a new favorite genre of spicy romance. Wanting to spread her imaginative wings and share her passions for teaching, empowering, and storytelling, NANDER put her knowledge and creativity to paper. Now a mother, wife, and proud indie author, NANDER brings her genre-hopping, rule-bending preferences to the table in original written works.

www.NANDER.co

www.ingramcontent.com/pod-product-compliance
Lightning Source LLC
LaVergne TN
LVHW051246040225
802862LV00003B/5